"I hardly slept last night," Sandra explained. Then in a rush she said, "If there hadn't been this emergency with my father, I'd have been on my way to tell you I can't marry you. But now I'm stuck with you!"

"It might turn out better than you think."

"It will be a disaster!" Sandra said emphatically.

"Or a resounding success," he countered, looking quite unperturbed. "Why not wait and see?"

"Will nothing dent your arrogant belief that you know me better than I know myself?" she stormed.

"*Confident* belief, Sandra, not arrogant. Confident enough to believe that one day our marriage will be for real."

"Never!"

"That's a word I won't accept," he said.

ROBERTA LEIGH wrote her first book at the age of nineteen and since then has written more than seventy romance novels, as well as many books and film series for children. She has also been an editor of a woman's magazine and produced a teen magazine, but writing romance fiction remains one of her greatest joys. She lives in Hampstead, London, and has one son.

Books by Roberta Leigh

ROBERTA LEIGH

storm cloud marriage

Harlequin Books

TORONTO • NEW YORK • LONDON
AMSTERDAM • PARIS • SYDNEY • HAMBURG
STOCKHOLM • ATHENS • TOKYO • MILAN

Harlequin Presents first edition October 1988
ISBN 0-373-11115-0

Original hardcover edition published in 1987
by Mills & Boon Limited

CHAPTER ONE

'Why do you assume a man's only interested in me for my money?' Sandra Harris grumbled to her father, glancing round the elegant drawing-room and irritably tossing back her mane of tawny gold hair.

'*You're* the one who assumes it,' he replied, peering at her over his spectacles. 'Why else are you cagey with this Barry fellow? Scared he'll find you more desirable when he discovers you're the daughter of Harris Pharmaceuticals?'

'My identity won't make the slightest difference to him.'

'Then why dress like a rag-bag to hide it?'

Sandra grinned as she looked down at her layered green skirt and top. 'This rag-bag happens to be a Kenzo and costs the earth! But it's Barry we're discussing, not me, and I'd like you to meet him.'

'Then you're going to tell him who you are?'

Sandra nodded. She was crazy not to have done it before. Now he might well think she didn't trust him—which wasn't true.

'Invite him whenever you like,' Edward Harris went on. 'Though if I don't take to him, I'll show it. You've a lot to offer a man, you know, and I don't only mean money.'

'You're biased, darling.' She leaned over and kissed the top of his head. He only wanted the best for her—trouble was, his 'best' was Randall Pearson, a man she disliked intensely despite his apparent virtues being rammed down her throat—or probably because of it!

'Pearson the Paragon', as she privately dubbed him, was second-in-command of the company Edward Harris had built into one of the largest in the world. Well bred, well educated, and well off in his own right, he had joined it from one of their main competitors, and had quickly become Managing Director.

'I thank the day Randall joined me.' Her father seemed to have divined her thoughts. 'I'd be hard put to it replacing him if he left.'

'Why should he? He knows which side his bread is buttered—and jammed, too!'

'It was buttered and jammed long before he came to me. It took me a year to entice him from Goodhews. He's not only a brilliant executive, he's an outstanding analytical chemist.'

True, but who cared? The very mention of the man gave her a mental attack of hives. Still, she was ready to admit she was unreasonable where he was concerned. If her father hadn't thrown him at her as a suitable husband from the time she was sixteen, she might have found him tolerable. But knowing he was regarded as a surrogate son had made her react against him. Indeed, getting away from Randall had been her main reason for going to art school in London, instead of the excellent one in Norwich, her home town.

She had thoroughly enjoyed college life, particularly as it had freed her from her father's stifling protectiveness.

'I want to make it on my own,' she had informed him when he had offered to buy a studio and gallery for her after she graduated. 'Anyway, I don't have the talent to be the sort of painter you're thinking of.'

'The landscape you did for my birthday was excellent.'

'You're a teeny weeny bit biased,' she had grinned. 'It was nothing more than competent, believe me.'

'So what are you going to do, then?'

'Graphic art. I thought I'd try for a job in advertising.'

'Robbins and Dean will be delighted to have you. I'll give them a call.'

'You'll do nothing of the sort! I want to get a job on my own merit, Daddy, not yours.'

And on her merit it was, for Barry Chadwick, an account executive with Causten Advertising, whom she met at a party a week later, had considered her very merit-worthy indeed, and engaged her on the spot.

Discovering he was barking up the wrong tree, which she was quick to point out the first day she started working for him, he accepted the rebuff with good humour, and not until several months had passed and he had already rewarded her design skill with a substantial rise, did he ask her out.

He was quite different from most of the men she dated, who either hailed from her own monied circle, with attitudes to correspond, or were hard-up art graduates. But Barry, while having his feet firmly on the ground, had his sights fixed on the stars. Getting to the top was his prime ambition, and he was intelligent and hard-working enough to be well on the way there.

Their relationship had developed with a speed that had astonished them both, though Sandra was the one to hold back, for Barry, though happy to see her every spare moment he had, was cagey when talking of their future. And though he fancied her like mad, 'love' didn't appear to be in his vocabulary.

However, it hadn't been in Randall's either, and he had asked her to marry him! Strange she should think of it now, when it had happened four years ago, but the memory of it was as clear as if it were yesterday.

The night had been warm and her excitement high—induced by two glasses of champagne and several dances with a handsome young neighbour Sandra hadn't seen since she was fourteen! Leaving him for a moment to fetch a handkerchief from her room, she was hurrying across the hall when Randall waylaid her.

Impeccable in white dinner-jacket and black trousers that emphasised his physique, his pale grey eyes—behind his heavy-rimmed spectacles—regarded her unblinkingly.

'Hello, Sandra. Enjoying yourself?'

'Very much. And you?'

He nodded, the light catching the sleek fawn hair brushed shiny as satin. 'I'll enjoy it more when the other band comes and I can ask you to dance—reggae isn't my kind of music!'

So what else was new? But she was delighted to hear it. The last thing she wanted was to be stuck with him!

'The band won't be changing for ages,' she said brightly. 'I only let Daddy book it so his friends wouldn't feel left out of things.'

'I wasn't talking of a minuet!' Randall said with unexpected humour, and touched her lightly on the arm. 'May I have a word with you in private?'

Short of being rude, she couldn't refuse, and, stifling her impatience, she preceded him into her father's study.

What on earth did he want? Impatiently she tapped one small, silk-shod foot as he went to stand by the fireplace.

'You're leaving for college on Monday, I believe,' he said conversationally.

'Yes.'

'Then I'm glad I can speak to you tonight. I'm going abroad for a while, and this is the only chance I'll have of seeing you until your holidays.'

So what? she thought irritably. She hardly saw him anyway. She inched towards the door, stopping as she saw his hand go to his pocket and take out a small purple box. Her puzzlement vanished. He only wanted to give her her birthday present. Trust Randall to make a big production of it!

'A little birthday gift,' he confirmed, holding it out. 'I didn't want to put it with the others in the hall.'

Certain it was bound to be as boring and conventional as the man himself, she gave a false smile and opened the box with pretended eagerness.

Just as she had imagined, and as far removed from her taste as a pork pie from a Muslim! On a bed of black velvet lay a hand-painted miniature of an exquisite young girl with eyes and hair the colour of Sandra's. Rubies and seed pearls encrusted the gold edge, as also the clasp of the fine gold chain.

Involuntarily Sandra put a hand to the brightly coloured glass necklace at her throat. She had fallen in love with it at Kensington Market a few days ago. The contrast nearly made her laugh! Holding it in check, and still staring at the pendant, she said, 'It's charming. Thank you very much.'

She hoped she had not come across too flat. She glanced at Randall. One never knew with him. He rarely showed much expression, while she herself was an open book.

'I'm glad you like it,' he answered tonelessly, and as their eyes met, she thought his pale as silver.

'I'd like you to accept it as a combined birthday and engagement present,' he went on. 'It seemed premature to buy a ring until you've given me your answer.'

Speechlessly she stared at him.

'I'm asking you to marry me,' he added.

He couldn't be serious! But his expression showed he was, and the very idea infuriated her into replying, 'We hardly know each other. I've never even been out with you!'

'We've known each other two years; I've seen you most times I've dined here.'

'I see Thomas every day,' she rejoined, referring to the butler, 'but I don't expect him to propose to me!'

Randall's total stillness was his only sign of annoyance. 'Hardly the same thing, my dear. Though perhaps I should have made my intentions clearer. It's simply that your going off to art school came as a surprise and I didn't want to lose you.'

'Me or the Harris dynasty?' she flared. 'I know exactly why you want to marry me, and it's got nothing to do with love.'

'You're very sure.'

'Actions speak louder than words, and yours can hardly be called loverlike!'

For several seconds Randall remained silent, the increasing pallor of his already pale skin the only a sign of anger. 'I don't need to marry to secure a dynasty, Sandra, I'm quite capable of securing my own.'

'Come off it,' she retorted. 'This company is ready made for you.'

'What makes you certain I *don't* love you?' he countered, ignoring her comment.

'The way you've behaved to me—as I said, you've never even asked me out.'

'A mistake, I agree. But only because I thought you too young to——'

'But mature enough to be your wife,' she cut in sarcastically. 'Or do you have a fetish for child brides?'

Unexpectedly he laughed. 'I don't blame you for being angry, and I understand why. Actually I intended laying siege to you slowly, and was only precipitated into action by your decision to leave home.'

Lay siege to her, eh? Precipitated into action? Holy cow! Had anyone ever received a less romantic proposal?

'The answer's no. I could never marry you. Your idea of love isn't mine.'

One finely shaped eyebrow rose quizzically. 'What *is* your idea of love?'

'It's passion and caring. Wanting someone so much you're only half alive when you're not with them! I can't imagine *you* having those emotions about anyone, Randall. You're too cold and contained.'

'Think so?'

Before she knew it, he pulled her into his arms and his mouth came down hard and warm on hers. For an instant, astonishment held her motionless, but as she started struggling his searching hands stopped her, moving along her back to mould her body to his. His fingers caressed the rounded curve of her hips, the swell of her buttocks, and she gave a convulsive shiver and ran her tongue along the edge of his lips, lapping them like a kitten milk.

Expecting a response from him, she was amazed when he abruptly dropped his hands and stepped away from her. Bewildered, she tried to gather herself together, his composure making her feel she had behaved like a silly schoolgirl. But she'd show him she wasn't!

'What were you trying to prove?' she sneered. 'That you're as good at kissing as everything else you do?'

'*Have* I proved it?'

'Of course. And it's what I expected. You're an excellent businessman, and I'm just another piece of business to you! Only there's one thing you've forgotten.'

'Which is?'

'That I can't be bought or taken over! Now if you don't mind, my *friends* are waiting for me.'

Turning on her heel, she stalked out.

Only next day did she remember the miniature. But when she went to the library for it, it had gone, and she was too embarrassed to call Randall and ask if he had taken it back. She assumed he had, and a month later was proved right for, returning from art school for the weekend, she found a package of six video cassettes of her favourite pop groups waiting for her, with a birthday card from him.

'When are you going back to London?' Her father broke into her reverie as he picked up the Sunday papers.

'Pretty soon. I've a date this evening.'

At least she hoped she had. Her father's remarks had made her decide to be truthful with Barry. She would invite him out—somewhere really special—and take the plunge.

Hurrying to her room, she put through a call to him.

'Barry? Doing anything tonight?'

'No, why?'

'I'm taking you to dinner.'

'How come?' he queried.

'I've something important to tell you.'

'You're whetting my appetite!'

'Which is why I suggested dinner,' she laughed.

'Then buzz me when you're back and I'll collect you.'

'No need. I'll change here and call for you on my way into town. I won't bother going back to my apartment first.'

'I wish you'd say you won't bother going back *afterwards.*'

Laughing, Sandra put down the receiver. She wasn't laughing inside, though. Far from it. Since Mario, sex had been no laughing matter to her. She had tried to tell Barry about him, but always, at the last minute, had chickened out. Perhaps when he asked her to marry him she would find the courage, but at the moment it was an episode she wanted to forget. She frowned. Who was she kidding? She could no more forget what Mario had done to her than she could her own name!

CHAPTER TWO

DECIDING to pull out the stops for her date with Barry, Sandra exchanged what her father called her 'rag-bag clothes' for a silky black Armani which emphasised the grace of her tall, slender body and tiny waist.

She was also heavier with her make-up, using blusher on her high cheekbones, and mascara to darken lashes long and thick as a Barbie doll's. She wound her hair atop her head instead of wearing it loose. Thick and shiny, it was the colour of wild honey, and matched eyes that tilted at the corners, giving her a faintly exotic appearance which men found irresistible.

On her way to the garage, she decided against using her second-hand Renault in favour of the scarlet Mercedes coupé her father had bought her for her last birthday. She had not yet taken it to London, knowing it would destroy her image of a hardworking girl living on her salary! But as she was going to blow the secret anyway, she might as well knock Barry back with two feathers instead of one!

Two hours later she was ringing the bell of his smart mews house, her heart doing its usual flip-flop as he opened the door and smiled down at her, a six-foot hunk of black-haired, bronze-skinned masculinity, handsome enough to feature in the very commercials he made for television.

'Hi, beautiful.' His brown eyes crinkled at the corners.

'Hi, good-looking!' She longed to fling herself into his arms but instead followed him into a living-room that might have come straight out of *House & Garden*—black carpet, red-lacquered walls, black and white furniture.

13

'Care for a drink?' he asked, sauntering to an Art Deco cabinet.

'No, thanks. I'll wait till we're out. I've booked a table at the Connaught.'

His glass stopped half-way to his mouth. 'Your important news must be *very* important.'

'It is.' She eyed his casual slacks and silk sweater. 'Quit talking and get changed.'

He downed his whisky, then with a swift movement peeled off his sweater. Sandra swallowed hard, resisting the urge to touch his golden skin and rippling muscles.

'Come and talk to me while I dress.' He held out a hand to her.

'No—I'll distract you, and then we'll be late.'

'Sounds a marvellous reason for being late!' His eyes were teasing. 'No?'

'No!'

With a chuckle he disappeared into the bedroom, though he did not chuckle when he stepped into the mews with her and she pranced ahead of him to her Mercedes.

'This is the news?' he asked, walking around it as admiringly as a peacock a hen. 'I didn't know I gave you such a big rise last month!'

'You didn't,' she quipped, sliding behind the wheel.

He said no more and neither did she, aware of him eyeing her speculatively as they drove the short distance to the hotel.

Entering the wood-panelled lobby, Sandra felt a sense of homecoming. This was her father's favourite hotel, where he stayed when he had to be in London overnight, and the two-bedroomed suite on the third floor had over the years, seen her transition from schoolgirl to self-possessed young woman.

The porter welcomed her with a beaming smile, and the desk clerk—busy on the telephone—permitted himself a discreet lift of the hand as she moved down the narrow, mirror-lined corridor to the dining room.

The head waiter was off duty but John, the man who normally served them, was there to greet her.

'Quite a while since I've seen you, Miss Harris.'

'Only a couple of months,' she told him.

'I trust Mr Harris is well?'

'Couldn't be better.' She followed him to her usual table by the wall and sat down, avoiding Barry's eyes as he took the seat opposite. 'What do you recommend tonight, John?'

'We've excellent baby lobster flown in from Scotland yesterday. Grilled with butter, they can't be improved on.'

'Sounds great. Lobster OK for you, Barry?'

He nodded, and she ordered two, then asked to see the wine waiter, entering into a spirited discussion with him before settling on a fairly dry vintage champagne to see them through their meal. Only as he moved off did she lean back and look squarely at Barry's astounded face.

'OK,' he said. 'You've made your point. So who are you? Getty's granddaughter?'

'Not quite.'

His eyes narrowed as he studied her, ranging from her dress to the gold circlet around her neck—simple enough to be genuine.

'Sandra Harris,' he mused. 'Harris Textiles? No, there are three sons, no daughters... The shoe company in Nottingham, perhaps?'

'Try again.'

'The only other Harris is the pharmaceutical group, and it couldn't...' He saw her expression and his mouth dropped. 'I see. No need to ask you why you kept quiet about it. Little Miss Rich Girl wants to be loved for herself.'

'Something like that.'

'Then why confess now?'

'I think you've known me long enough to value me for myself.'

'It's taken you until today to value *me*,' he retorted.

'Meaning?'

'That you didn't trust me enough to tell me who you were.'

'Please, Barry, try to see it from my angle,' begged Sandra. 'It's awful not knowing if a man's dating you because he likes you, or because he sees you as a meal ticket! And then some men are the exact opposite. They won't ask you out because they're scared you'll expect more than they can afford.'

'What a tough life you've had!' he jeered.

'There is no need to be sarcastic. I'd give anything to be an ordinary girl who——'

'It isn't your money that stops you being ordinary,' he cut in, 'it's your talent. You're a marvellous graphic designer, though whether you remain one—with your bank balance—is another matter.'

'Leave my bank balance out of it!' she said crossly.

'I wish I could.' He rubbed the side of his jaw. 'I'm sorry to sound off like this, but you've given me a hell of a jolt. An hour ago I was an important account executive in love with his assistant. Now I'm simply a guy in advertising, and you're heiress to a fortune.'

'I'm still *me*. For goodness' sake don't let my stupid money come between us.'

'Money, stupid? That shows the difference between us!' He shook his head. 'I still can't take in who you are.'

But as their meal progressed and the champagne took effect, Barry grew less defensive, and Sandra started filling him in on her family and background, trying to make him see it had begun as an ordinary middle class one.

'I still can't see myself being welcomed with open arms,' Barry pronounced. 'I bet your old man's got a duke lined up for you!'

'Daddy's not like that. He accepts people for what they are, and you're intelligent, ambitious and top in your field.'

'He'll still regard me as a fortune-hunter.'

'Don't be silly.' Colour stained her cheeks, and he threw her a sardonic glance.

'I'd have been more inclined to believe you if you'd told me the truth about yourself before,' he reiterated.

'I've explained why I didn't. And your present attitude shows me I was right.'

He sighed. 'You can't blame me for being put off. I mean, what future is there for us? You're one of the super-rich and I'm an ordinary guy who's struggled to get where he is. I may not have achieved much by your reckoning, but I'm proud of what I've done and I don't want anyone looking down on me.'

'Why do you think I would?' she asked tearfully. 'I'm no different from the girl you took out Thursday night.'

'Yes, you are. You've shed your disguise, and it's bound to affect your attitude.'

Oh God, she thought, this whole scene's becoming a nightmare. Nothing was turning out as she had planned, and her future with Barry seemed to be disappearing into the land of never-never. Of course it was only his pride making him difficult. Despite his talk of men and women being equal, he liked being the one to give favours—easy to do when your girlfriend was also your assistant and relied on you for her job; another story entirely when said girl could buy you and your agency a hundred times over! Stupid of her not to have realised it. But then she had seen things from her point of view only, and not from the vantage of a handsome man used to having women at his beck and call. It isn't my money he objects to, she knew with dismal clarity, it's the power he thinks it gives me.

'I love you, Barry.' She threw pride to the wind.

'And I love you.'

The words were right, but the tone wasn't, and she didn't know what else to say to ease his mind. Only time would do that. Time and her own determination to show him she was the same hardworking, ambitious girl he had asked to work for him six months ago.

The only ray of sunshine in this gloomy scenario was that Barry's reaction would delight her father, who'd never be able to accuse him of being a fortune-hunter.

'Come home with me next weekend,' she said.

'I don't think so.'

'Please.'

'OK. But do me a favour and steer the conversation away from chemistry. It's my worst subject!'

'How's your snooker?' asked Sandra.

'Last time I played, I ripped the baize!'

She giggled, and he signalled for the bill.

'It's *my* treat, remember,' she protested, stopping abruptly as she saw him scowl.

'I can afford to pay for our dinner—even at the Connaught!'

She gave in instantly and followed him to the car, handing him the keys as she did.

'Sure you want me to?' he asked.

'Please. I find the Renault easier to handle.'

It was a lie in a good cause, for his face brightened as he took the wheel.

Neither of them made conversation, and because she felt she was treading on eggshells where he was concerned, Sandra did not break the silence. It was not until they were cruising down Knightsbridge that Barry's hand came down to lightly stroke her thigh. She trembled, and the tightening of his grip showed he had noticed, though she was disappointed when he returned his hand to the wheel.

Once in his apartment it was another story. Pushing the door shut with his foot, he reached hungrily for her. Never the gentlest of lovers, tonight—as if to prove he was still in control—he was rougher, his mouth fierce on hers, his tongue insistent as it harshly probed the soft inner moistness.

Passion flared deep inside her and she pressed closer to him, resenting the barrier of clothing separating them. Sensing it, he drew away and pulled her towards the bedroom.

Instantly the old fear took over.

'No, Barry! I can't!'

'Why not? I want you, sweetheart, and you sure as hell want *me*. So why play games?'

'It's no game. Sex is special, and I don't want you to rush me.'

'Rush you? Dammit, we've known each other six months!' he protested.

'Four of which you were otherwise engaged,' Sandra pointed out.

'Let's concentrate on the last two. I've seen no one else except you, and if you meant what you said at dinner tonight, you'd be urging *me* into bed. Or are you only amusing yourself with me? As you are with a job you don't need, earning money you don't want?'

'That's a horrible thing to say! If you think I'm that kind of person, you can't love me very much.'

'And you can't love *me*, if you keep holding me off.'

He reached for her again, but she side-stepped him. 'No, Barry, I won't!'

'Why not? Got a hang-up about sex?'

Here was her chance to come clean about Mario, but as her lips parted, she stopped. She had given Barry enough to think about for one evening without adding to it by disclosing the trauma of her past.

'It's—it's something like that,' she hedged. 'I was brought up to believe it wrong to go to bed with a man unless you're married to him.'

'Then you'll never go to bed with *me*, sweetheart. Marriage is one commitment I've no intention of making.'

'If you love me——'

'I do. But marriage is out.'

'Why?'

'Because it doesn't mean anything to me. My parents fought like cat and dog till my old man walked out, and my two sisters are divorced.'

'That doesn't mean *we* can't be happy,' Sandra protested.

'It does in my book. I've seen too many couples who've lived together happily start hating each other the minute they tied the knot. I'm sorry, Sandra, but if it's a husband you want, you'd better look elsewhere.'

'You think I can turn my love off like a tap?'

'Of course not. I'm just laying it on the line for you.' He came close to her. 'If you're worried your father won't like us living together, don't tell him till he gets to know me better.'

'He'd never approve.'

'Hard cheese. It's your life, not his, and no one can dictate how you live it.'

'You're letting your parents' experience dictate *yours*,' she accused, voice trembling. She had been on cloud nine an hour ago; now she was tumbling off it.

'This is getting us nowhere,' Barry scowled, 'and I won't lie to get you into bed.' His face softened as he saw the glitter of her tears. 'You know I love you, darling. Just let me hold you. I promise I won't do more.'

His gentle persuasiveness was nearly her undoing; probably would have been if excited arousal hadn't made his tongue resume its aggressive probing of her mouth. Fright took hold of her again, and she pushed him violently away.

'No!' she cried. 'I won't go to bed with you on your terms—not ever!'

'Then we'd best call it a day and part while we're still friends.'

Had he spoken with anger Sandra might have put up a fight, but he was so nonchalant she felt he didn't care if he never saw her again.

Silently she went into the hall, waiting for him to stop her. But he merely followed, leaning against the wall and watching her as she put on her coat.

It can't be ending like this, she thought. Yet pride would not let her grovel. If he didn't love her for what she was, to hell with him!

Head high, she went to the door. 'I'm sorry it's ended like this, Barry.'

'Me, too. Spoiled little rich girls can't have everything they want.'

'Nor can spoiled men!'

His mouth lifted in a lopsided grin. 'You're right. We're both right, in fact.'

She waited for him to continue, and when he didn't, opened the door and stalked out.

Returning to her apartment on the top floor of a terraced house near Campden Hill Square, Sandra relived the whole acrimonious scene. Neither of them had come out of it well. Her reluctance to discuss Mario, who was the reason for her sexual hang-up, was as much a sign of emotional immaturity as Barry's citing his parents' unhappy marriage as a reason for staying single.

She stopped at a traffic light. Hurt though she was by his behaviour, life without him was untenable. Perhaps if they lived together happily for a while he would judge their relationship on its own merit and not on that of his parents and sisters. It was a chance worth taking, especially as the alternative didn't bear thinking of.

Should she call and tell him of her change of heart, or leave it till tomorrow? No, let him stew till she saw him in the office. She'd probably confess about Mario too. Yes, definitely. It was important there were no secrets between them.

Outwardly calm but inwardly full of trepidation, Sandra went to the agency next morning. She couldn't wait to tell Barry of her change of heart, but luck was against her, for he was out with a client.

He did not return until late morning, by which time she was in session with the art director, and it was noon before she was free. Anxious to catch him before he disappeared for lunch, she darted down the corridor to his office and, rushing in, was disconcerted to find another man with him.

'The very girl I want!' Barry waved a hand at her. 'I'd like you to meet Mr Arnie Jackson, Publicity Director of Marriot Tights. He likes the layouts you've done for the autumn campaign.'

' "Likes" is putting it mildly. They're sensational!'

Arnie Jackson's foxy eyes roamed Sandra's body, making her wonder if a man existed who didn't mentally undress a girl when he first met her!

'What about my taking you both to lunch?' he went on.

'Sure.' Barry gave Sandra a look that said she had better say yes, and another half-hour found the three of them seated in a crowded Soho *trattoria*, conferring on the virtues of ladies' tights as opposed to stockings.

'A girl with your looks should be showing them, not drawing them,' Mr Jackson leered at Sandra between shovelling pasta into his mouth. 'Ever considered modelling?'

'Only in clay.'

Ignoring her joke, he inched his chair closer to hers and poured the remains of the Chianti into his glass. 'Come on, Barry, tell Sandra what we've dreamed up for the television commercials.'

'It'll have to wait till I get back Thursday.' Barry glanced at his watch. 'I'm catching the two-fifteen to Leeds, and if I don't get a move on I'll miss it.'

Sandra was dismayed. 'I didn't know you were going away.'

'I didn't know it myself till this morning.'

'I'll come with you to the station.' Maybe she could talk to him en route.

He nodded and pushed back his chair. 'Sorry I have to rush, Arnie. I'll see you next Monday. Meanwhile I'll have Sandra do a few other layouts.'

Alone with her in the taxi, Barry grinned broadly. 'You made quite a hit with Arnie! Had him eating out of your hand.'

'He'd like to have nibbled a bit more,' she snorted. 'What a nauseating character!'

'You get nauseated too easily,' he told her.

'If you mean last night, then——'

'I don't. But if the cap fits...'

'It doesn't. That's what I want to talk to you about. I——'

'Keep it till I get back,' he cut in as the taxi drew into Paddington. Leaning forward, he kissed the tip of her nose. 'You're still my favourite girl.'

'Honestly?'

'Cross my heart. I couldn't manage without you.'

He disappeared into the ticket hall before she could ask whether he meant at work or personally, and dejectedly returned to the agency.

She found it hard going to concentrate the next few days, and she counted the hours till Thursday and Barry's return. But her hopes were dashed when she arrived at the office and Bob Wallace, another account executive and Barry's closest friend, informed her he would not be back till the following day.

'I spoke to him an hour ago and he's staying over to see another client.'

He might have let me know, Sandra thought crossly, and instinctively felt he wanted her to eat a goodly portion of humble pie before they made up. But it had never been her favourite dessert, and she wasn't about to sample it now, which he'd learn to his cost.

Her temper lasted till next day, and when Barry hadn't put in an appearance by the evening, she pocketed her pride and telephoned him at home.

No answer. She chewed on her nails. He was either catching a later train or staying north for the weekend. Come to think of it, he had family there. Still, he was bound to return Sunday at the latest, for they had an early meeting on Monday with the dreadful Arnie Jackson.

Meanwhile the weekend loomed emptily ahead of her. Should she go home or stay here on the off-chance of Barry returning on Saturday? It was no contest, and Barry won hands down. She wanted to set the record straight between them, and would have no peace until she did.

But a seven a.m. call on Sunday from Mrs Helmer, her father's housekeeper, shattered her plans.

'You'd best come down at once, Miss Sandra. Mr Harris was taken ill during the night, and——'

'I'm on my way!'

Crashing down the receiver, Sandra dressed, threw a few clothes into a case, and was half out of the door when she dashed back to call Bob Wallace and tell him her news.

'I'm not sure when I'll be in the office—depends how things go. Will you let Barry know for me?'

'Sure. Though you can do it yourself. He came back last night. We spent the evening together.'

Sandra's stomach lurched. Barry was home, yet hadn't bothered to inform her! Anger and longing for him warred with anxiety for her father, but anxiety won and, muttering to Bob that she hadn't time to speak to Barry, she ran down to her car.

The traffic was thin, this being a cold, wet Sunday, and she was soon out of London and belting across flat, uninteresting landscape. The further east she travelled, the colder it became—the grey sky matching her mood, the occasional mournful cry of a seagull echoing the hollowness in her heart. Not only was she worried sick about her father, but Barry too. Whoever had said love was sweet hadn't met a nineteen-eighties man who ran a mile from marriage!

The sign pointing to Lillingham headed her inland again, her spirits rising as the village church came in sight, then the High Street. Half a mile further, she turned through massive gates into the driveway winding to the large old mansion that had always been home to her; a home without the homeliness of a woman's touch. Strange her father hadn't remarried. Her mother had died when she was born, and as far as she knew, he hadn't looked at another woman since, devoting his life to business and his daughter—in that order.

Happily she had basked in his attention until her late teens, when it had dawned on her that he was grooming her to eventually take his place. It had seemed a fate worse than death, and with the hyperbole of the young she had made it plain she had her own plans. Art school being one of them.

Fortuitously Randall Pearson had appeared on the scene, and the ease with which he had superseded her in her father's business sights had occasionally made her wonder if this was why she disliked him. Not that she had ever actually fancied him! They were too disparate: he cold where she was warm, analytical where she was intuitive, reserved where she was impulsive.

Wideacres rose in front of her, and as she stopped outside the brass-studded oak door, Thomas the butler appeared, his expression grave.

Jumping from the car, she dashed over to him. 'Is he——'

'He's holding his own, Miss Sandra.'

With a heartfelt sigh, she went upstairs, pausing outside her father's door to compose herself. Then forcing a smile, she went in.

'You must have driven like the devil to get here so soon!'

Edward Harris's gruff tones and familiar humour sent a wave of relief washing over her, though it ebbed as she moved nearer and saw the greyness of his skin. He was propped up with pillows, and Ralph Baxter, the family doctor, was seated beside him.

She bent to kiss her father's cheek. 'How are you, darling?'

'Fine.' He threw an irate glance at the other man. 'Ralph wanted me to go to hospital, but I wouldn't. He likes nothing better than to fuss.'

'And you like nothing better than working yourself into the ground,' came the testy response. 'You won't take any notice of me, so perhaps you'll listen to the specialist.'

'Depends what he says!' Edward Harris looked back at his daughter. 'How long you staying?'

'Till you're up and about.'

'That's one way to keep me bedridden!'

She laughed. 'Then I'll limit myself to a month.' She squeezed his hand gently and spoke to the doctor. 'When's the specialist coming?'

'In about an hour. I was lucky to get him today.'

'It could have waited till Monday,' Edward Harris grunted.

'Stop talking and rest,' ordered Ralph Baxter.

Surprisingly he did, and Sandra glanced at him, mouthed to the doctor that she was going to unpack, and tiptoed out.

As she went to her room, it suddenly hit her that her father was an old man. He was so vigorous that she had never given his age a thought. But at seventy, the strain of business must have taken its toll. She wondered if his reluctance to relinquish the reins entirely had to do with her refusal to marry Randall. Certainly their marriage would have kept the running of the company in the family, something which meant a great deal to him.

'Mr Pearson's downstairs, Miss Sandra.' Thomas appeared at the head of the stairs.

'My father can't see anyone,' she said firmly.

'Mr Pearson wishes to have a word with *you*.'

Typical of him! Smelling death, he was hovering like a vulture. 'I'm in no mood to talk to anyone, Thomas. Please make my apologies to him and say I'll call him as soon as I have any news.'

Entering her room, Sandra found her case unpacked, and she hovered uncertainly for a few seconds, then peered through the window to make sure Randall's car had gone before going down to the garden-room.

A log fire burned in the grate and she drew a chair closer to it, determined not to give way to self-pity. It was hard not to, for when her father died she would be totally alone. 'Rich in money, poor in friends.' The phrase rang through her mind, and she sighed, accepting that she had no one to blame but herself.

In electing to go to art school, she had followed a life so different from those of her school friends that she had lost touch with them. Not that she had cared at the time—or even now, come to think of it!—for her boarding school had been a cloistered one, its snobby pupils hailing from the pampered background of old money and country estates. Surprising that a man like her father—self-made and proud of it—had sent her to such a place. He had probably considered it a protected environment.

Yet she had drifted away from her artist friends too, though this had been *force majeure*, many of them scattering across the country in search of work, and those in London content to 'starve in a garret' until they had proved themselves, while she—rich enough to buy them a thousand times over—had set aside her artistic ambitions and concentrated on showing her father she was capable of earning a living.

But the itch to put her talent to the test—her innermost talent rather than her slick ability as a graphic designer—still nagged at her, and it was stronger than ever as she wandered round the room and looked at the watercolours gracing the walls. It was not a medium that had ever appealed to her, but today it did, and she decided to go to Norwich next morning and buy paints, brushes and paper.

She had promised to stay here as long as she was needed, and must ask Dr Baxter if she should think in terms of weeks or months. Fear clutched at her again. If the worst happened, who could she turn to, rely on?

Oh, Barry! she cried silently, why did we have that stupid quarrel? If you were here now you could have me on any terms you liked, as long as I knew we would always be together.

CHAPTER THREE

THE specialist confirmed that Edward Harris had suffered a severe heart attack and would have to take life far easier in future.

'Short of putting him in a strait-jacket,' Sandra exclaimed, 'I don't see how we can make him do it! He thrives on activity and challenge.'

'He won't thrive for long if he doesn't rethink his lifestyle,' came the answer.

All very well for the specialist to say, but how best to handle a man who was used to giving orders, not obeying them? Sandra was frowning over this as she returned to his room.

'Don't look so woebegone!' her father said. 'I'm not dead yet. Now where in hell is Randall? I can't understand why he hasn't been to see me.'

'He was here earlier, but didn't want to disturb you.'

'It disturbs me more not seeing him! He's good company, Sandra. I wish you two were friends.'

'We are,' she lied.

'Not the kind I'd like. If only——'

'—you'd stop talking,' she finished for him. 'If you don't, Nurse will send me away.'

'That's just what I'm going to do!' the nurse smiled, coming in from the dressing-room. 'Time for your rest, Mr Harris.'

'I'm not tired,' he grunted.

'Then close your eyes and lie quiet.'

'Looks as if you've met your match, Dad,' Sandra chuckled from the door. 'I'm going for a walk.'

Once outside the house, she regretted it. It was cold enough to freeze her breath, and the damp seemed to penetrate her bones. Abandoning her intention of making for the copse, she headed down the drive, and was nearing the gates when she heard the purr of an engine. Its restrained power brought Randall to mind, and she was wryly amused when a silver-grey sports car glided to a stop beside her, and the man himself stepped neatly from it.

'Hello, Sandra.' As usual his soft voice was devoid of expression. 'I called earlier, but Thomas said your father was asleep.'

'He isn't allowed visitors,' she said curtly. 'The specialist doesn't want him bothered with business.'

'That goes without saying.'

Randall's tone remained unchanged. Anyone else would have resented her attitude, but not this paragon!

'I'll tell him you called,' she went on.

'Thank you.' Behind his heavy-rimmed spectacles his eyes glittered cold as the winter sky. 'Want a lift to the house?' he asked unexpectedly, opening the passenger-seat door.

'No, thanks.'

'It's beginning to rain.'

Ungraciously Sandra slid in beside him. His seat was pushed further back than hers, making her realise how tall he was—funny she hadn't noticed it before! Nor what aesthetic looks he had! Yet she knew this was deceptive for, calling in at the office some months ago, she had caught him in his shirt sleeves, whip-cord muscles visible through the linen.

But then there was a great deal that was deceptive about this man: the calm, the faint drawl, the languid manner; all of which had to disguise a ferocious, driving energy. How else could he have reorganised entire departments of the company almost single-handedly?

'Will you be staying home long?' he broke the silence.

'As long as my father needs me.'

'Permanently, then?'

'Very funny! You know exactly what I mean.'

'Yes. But I often wonder if *you* do.'

She was still puzzling over this when they reached the house. She clambered out quickly before he went round to open the door for her, and was irritated when he strode up the steps without making any attempt to do so.

'I told you, you can't see my father!' she stormed, racing after him.

'I only want to send him a note.'

'If it's about business . . .'

'It's to wish him better.'

Deflated, Sandra went into the drawing-room, his step quiet behind her, putting her in mind of a leopard on the prowl. 'Don't you ever lose your temper?' she asked petulantly.

'Not since I was a child.'

He said no more, which didn't surprise her, for he rarely spoke of his family or background. All she knew of him was that he was a brilliant chemist and a first-class executive.

'Mind if I help myself to a drink?' he asked, and at her shrug poured himself a whisky and soda.

She watched him, aware that she was trembling. It had to be from anger, for the mere sight of him set her hackles rising. Why didn't he leave her alone? Yet as long as she remained single, he'd try to safeguard his position by marrying her. Pity she didn't understand the ramifications of the company and the family trust. She hadn't a clue how many shares her father had put in her name, or whether Randall had a sufficient holding to give him a significant say. As soon as her father was well enough, she would ask him.

She became aware of Randall staring at her. Was he admiring her legs or worrying about the company's re-

sults, due out next week? His bland expression made it
hard to tell.

Smoothing her skirt across her knees, she glanced at
him out the corner of her eye. He had now gone to stand
by the fire, and his features were etched against the red-
gold flames: the high forehead of an intellectual—a
comparison heightened by the horn-rimmed spectacles
that were as much a part of him as the sliver of gold
encircling his wrist, the slimmest watch in the world. His
nose, like his character, was firm and unyielding, chin
and mouth equally determined. A man not to be taken
lightly, she decided again.

As he sipped his whisky, the movement drew up the
sleeve of his dark grey jacket. Like everything he wore,
it was impeccably cut, and she'd bet a pound to a penny
his wardrobe was full of similar suits in sober colours,
with shelves full of creaseless white shirts and anon-
ymous ties. He probably even had his pyjamas hand-
tailored in Savile Row!

'What's amusing you?' he questioned, turning from
the fire.

'I was wondering if you were born in a dark suit! I
can't picture you as a baby.'

'Even Dracula was,' he said blandly.

'I think you were born with a test tube in one hand
and company accounts in the other!'

'Whereas you had a golden spoon and a paint-brush.'

She ignored this. 'We're oil and water, Randall. We'll
never mix.'

'Not unless we find the right emulsifier.'

'If you're getting technical...'

'Sorry.' His smile curled the edge of his mouth, and
he drained his drink. 'If you'd give me some writing
paper, I'll do that note.'

'Don't bother. If Daddy's awake, I'll let you see him
for a minute.'

'That's kind of you.'

'No need to be sarcastic!'

'I wasn't. I always mean what I say, Sandra. You should learn to take me at face value.'

'I might if I were able to read your face! But it's a poker one.'

With the faintest of smiles he accompanied her up the wide carpeted stairs. This house is so large, she thought, I'd rattle around in it like a pea in a pod if I lived here alone.

'Don't think morbid thoughts,' Randall chided.

'How do you know what I'm thinking?'

'You *don't* have a poker face!'

Refusing to smile, Sandra stopped outside her father's door, inched it open and peeped in before turning to the man at her side. 'Only a minute,' she whispered, then walked in ahead of him.

Edward Harris beamed when he saw Randall. 'I wondered if they'd let me see you. What with the nurse and Sandra, I'll be lucky if I'm allowed a newspaper!'

'Definitely not a newspaper!' Randall smiled. 'And if you're in a hurry to get well, you'd better do as you're told.'

'Twaddle! Come closer and tell me what's been happening.'

'Nothing. It's Sunday and the plant's closed!'

'Ah, so it is. Those pills Ralph gave me have muddled me. Sunday, you say? Then you'll stay to dinner, of course.'

'I'm afraid I can't. I'm dining with Crawthorpe,' Randall told him.

'Are you, indeed? So he's finally going to sell you that patent of his. If he raises his price, I think we——'

'No business,' Randall cut across him, 'or Sandra will turf me out.'

'Too right,' she muttered from the foot of the bed.

'You won't need to,' Randall said smoothly. 'When I make a promise I keep it.'

Accepting his word, she left them alone and went to her room. Oddly uneasy, she paced the floor.

If only she could see Barry, or at least talk to him. So what if he hadn't called her when he got back to London! There could be a a host of reasons, but none to stop her calling *him*.

Heart pounding, she did. The phone rang several times and she was on the verge of hanging up when he answered.

'Barry? It's Sandra.'

'What news of your father?' he asked without preamble.

'He's stable, but I can't leave him yet.'

'I didn't expect you to. We'll manage.'

'Don't get anyone to replace me,' she joked, meaning it.

'I wouldn't dare. You might buy Causten's and fire me!'

'That isn't funny.'

Her voice wobbled and, hearing it, he was instantly contrite. 'Sorry, angel. I've been in a foul mood all morning. Must be the weather.'

'Are you still angry with me for saying no the other night?'

'Why should I be? You're free to do as you like.'

'That's what I wanted to talk to you about,' she said eagerly. 'I've decided——'

'Not now,' he interrupted. 'I'm in the middle of a conference.'

'At home?'

'I've been out of town all week, remember? I'm trying to catch up. But what say I come and see you next weekend?'

'My father can't have visitors.'

'I was coming to see *you*,' came the huffy response. 'I assumed your house is big enough for a visitor not to disturb him.'

'He'd still know you were here,' she said, wondering how to explain away Randall and her father's hopes for her, without upsetting Barry. But she already had, as his next words confirmed.

'If I'm not good enough to be invited to your home, forget it.'

'Don't be silly!' she exclaimed. 'It's just that for the last six years my father's been flinging someone else at me, and——'

'So be a Daddy's girl and marry him!'

'Oh Barry, I——'

But the line was already dead and, hurt by his refusal to listen to her, Sandra glared at the receiver. She hadn't exactly been the soul of diplomacy, but surely he had enough sense to appreciate why she didn't want to buck her father's authority at this particular moment in time?

She reached for the telephone, then stopped. Why should she beg forgiveness when Barry hadn't even had the decency to call her as soon as Bob had told him of her father's attack?

Depressed, she took a shower, as always finding water balm to her spirit. Afterwards, in a red velvet housecoat that clung to her full breasts and narrow waist, she went down to the drawing-room.

The curtains were drawn and shaded lamps cast a soft glow over the paintings on the walls. Pity her father didn't appreciate them. But then she didn't appreciate chemistry! She paused beside a Constable, duly humbled at the comparison of her own work, then warmed her hands at the fire, wondering if Randall had left for his dinner. Which reminded her, she had eaten nothing all day and was starving. She'd ask Mrs Mathews to serve supper at once.

Her hand was on the bell when Randall walked in.

'I didn't realise you were still here,' she said, uncomfortably conscious of the sexy image she presented. Had she known she'd see him, she would have worn red flannel! Pugnaciously she tucked her hands into the pockets of her housecoat. 'I thought you were going out to dinner?'

'I lied. Crawthorpe's sold his patent to someone else.'

'You told my father——'

'I didn't want to worry him with the truth.'

'You're a consummate liar,' she said drily.

'All in a good cause.'

'No wonder he thinks you're bloody marvellous!' she said peevishly.

'He thinks you are too,' Randall smiled. 'Which is as it should be.'

'I'm glad you approve,' she snapped, then, aware of being unnecessarily rude, added by way of apology, 'It must have been quite a blow—losing the patent.'

'One can't win them all.'

'I thought you abhorred failure.'

'I abhor lack of effort. But I'd be a fool if I believed I could always win, and a bigger fool if I wasted time in regret.'

Wondering if this was a veiled reference to her refusal to marry him, Sandra turned her back on him and stared into the fire, hoping he would take the hint and go.

'Are you happy in London?' Silent as a cat he had come to stand beside her.

'Very—as I'm sure my father's already told you.'

With startling swiftness he spun her round to face him. 'Why do you dislike me, Sandra? Because I once asked you to marry me?'

'Oh, that!' she said indifferently, pulling free of him. 'I don't dislike you. I merely find you irritating.'

'Because I'm Pearson the Paragon?' As he saw her discomfiture, his mouth quirked. 'I'm well aware of your name for me.'

'I dreamed it up when I was a teenager,' she defended. 'I don't see you as a paragon any more.'

'How, then?'

'As someone who'll do anything to achieve success—even to marrying the boss's daughter!'

'I see.' He stepped further away from her. 'You still think I want to secure my position in the company?'

'Yes, I do.'

He met her gaze squarely, though the firelight glinting on his lenses made it impossible to see his eyes. 'If I told you I loved you, would you still give me the same answer?'

'Certainly.'

With the faintest of shrugs he sauntered to the door. 'I'll be in to see your father tomorrow evening.'

'Good,' she said automatically.

'Who's the consummate liar this time?' he asked drily.

The door swung shut behind him and she backed irritably away from the fire, so hot with the impotent rage Randall always aroused in her that she had no need of extra warmth!

CHAPTER FOUR

SEVERAL days passed with no word from Barry, and though Sandra understood why he was angry with her, she was dismayed that his pride should blind him to her emotional need of him at this stage in her life.

Apart from a long walk twice a day, and a brief trip to Norwich to buy some watercolours, she spent most of her days with her father and, not wanting him to talk too much, set up a table beside his bed and sketched the scenes she saw from his window.

'You're getting better all the time,' he commented one afternoon.

'I hope so. I never realised what a wonderful medium watercolour is.'

'Well, at least *some* good has come out of my heart attack! I don't feel so badly now for keeping you here.'

'You needn't feel badly at all. I'm enjoying being home.'

She was lying in her back teeth, of course, and was glad she had when Dr Baxter spoke to her alone later that day.

'I'm pleased you're staying on, Sandra,' he said. 'Without you here, there'd be no keeping your father from the office.'

'Maybe I'd better stick a paintbrush in his hand and introduce him to art!'

'Would do him the world of good! Do you know he's kept most of the drawings you did as a child? Showed them to me in the library last year. Every one of them marked on the back with your age.'

Deeply touched at hearing this, Sandra went in search of them as soon as Dr Baxter had gone. She found them in the bottom drawer of the library desk and, leafing through them, realised that although her father might have yearned for a son to carry on his company, his love for her had been unqualified.

It gave her such a deep sense of being loved that she was able to see many things more clearly, not the least being Barry's behaviour. It was only natural he should find it difficult to accept that the girl he loved was an heiress, and by behaving like a spoiled one she had made it even harder for him. Without further thought she dialled his number.

'Another five minutes and I'd have been calling *you*,' he said when he heard her voice. 'I was a swine the other day.'

'It was my fault too. If you're still free to come here for the weekend——'

'Unfortunately not,' he cut in. 'I've just this minute fixed up a presentation for a new client, and I'll be tied up.'

Sandra bit her lip. Was Barry being truthful or merely showing he wasn't going to run after her no matter how rich she was? Hell! There she went again, being paranoid about her money.

'When you coming back to town?' he asked.

'I'm not sure. Any chance of my working from here?'

'I doubt it. Clients like to liaise with you.'

'What's happening with Arnie Jackson?'

'His tights are still holding up! Actually I've got some pretty good artwork on them.'

'Oh? Who from?'

'A freelance.'

Sandra was reassured. Freelances were expensive, and Barry wouldn't want to employ them often.

'Would it help if I came to London for a day, and you briefed me on what's wanted?'

'No. I'd need you here for more than a day. Look, forget your work for a while and concentrate on your father.'

'Can you come here the weekend after next?' she asked.

'I'll let you know.'

It was not the most satisfactory answer, and she felt a niggle of fear as she hung up.

'Am I being paranoic?' she asked the room at large, and glimpsing herself in the mirror above the mantelpiece—tall, golden-haired, haughty—knew she projected an aura that could frighten men off. And all because of Mario, who had caused her to surround herself with a glass wall which no one knew was there until they tried to come close to her. The sooner she told Barry about him, the better. It was the only way of clearing the air between them.

This decision made, she went to see her father, debating how best to say she was going to London for a day or two.

'You're looking pleased with yourself,' he said as she perched on his bed. 'Had a painting accepted by the Royal Academy?'

'You and your wishful thinking!' she laughed.

'There's nothing wrong with wishing. If you'd let *me* plan your career, I'd have——'

'I wanted to show you I could stand on my own feet.'

'Which you've done—and very well too. But I wish those feet would now walk up the aisle to Randall!'

'What a one-track mind you have! He isn't my type, Daddy, and he's twelve years older than me.'

'So what? Thirty-four doesn't make him Methuselah. You need someone older to control you.'

'I'm a girl, not a filly!'

'They both respond to a firm hand.'

'He's got two,' she sniffed, 'and they're both on your company! He runs it as if he owns it.'

'And worries about it as if he owns it, too—which is what counts. You're darned unreasonable where he's concerned. He could go to any of my rivals and write his own ticket.'

'I'm sure he hasn't stayed with you out of altruism,' said Sandra drily.

'I wouldn't expect him to. He knows that eventually he'll take over from me, and I assure you I don't know anyone I can trust more. Give him a chance, girlie. I haven't pushed him at you these last few years because I know it sets you against him, but he's the right man for you and will make you happy.'

'We've nothing in common.'

'Sure you have. He likes the country—same as you— and he's interested in art.'

'You must be joking! He's never once talked about it.'

'When have you given him the chance? Soon as you see him you rush off as if your tail's on fire!'

Edward Harris was flushed with excitement, and Sandra could have kicked herself. Hadn't she heard Dr Baxter's warning, for heaven's sake?

'I appreciate how you feel,' she soothed, 'and short of marrying Randall, I'll do anything you want.'

'You mean it?'

'Absolutely.'

'Then be friends with him, and for the time being don't commit yourself to this Barry fellow.'

Damn! Now she couldn't say she was going to London for a couple of days. 'Very well,' she said aloud. 'But don't build up false hopes.'

'I'm not. But if you'd drop your childish antagonism to Randall you might get a surprise.' The grey head rested back on the pillow. 'Before you go to bed tonight, let me know how you got on.'

'Got on?' she queried.

'With Randall. I've invited him here this evening.'

With an effort Sandra hid her exasperation, but, changing for dinner, she fumed at the turn of events. The only way to circumvent another unwanted proposal—at her father's urging Randall was bound to ask her again—was to introduce him to Barry as soon as possible. Only then would he accept that she wasn't going to be talked into a loveless marriage, no matter how good it was for the company or her shares in it!

Meanwhile she was obliged to entertain him tonight. The thought was enough to put her off her food, and an impish desire to put him off *his* prompted her to take out one of her most outrageous dresses: a black sheath, split up the side to reveal one long, slender leg and thigh. About to don it, she changed her mind. The last thing she wanted was a chase around the settee, and the high-necked, long-sleeved Jean Muir she chose instead was more likely to soothe than arouse.

Randall was lounging in a chair, whisky in hand, as she came into the drawing-room, and he rose and came towards her.

'Hope you don't mind my not waiting for you,' he said, half lifting his glass, 'but I had a long, tiring argument with the Board.'

'You won, of course.'

'Thanks for the "of course".'

The teasing in his voice hinted at an intimacy she balked at, and she side-stepped him and went to the drinks tray. But he was there before her.

'Sherry? Dubonnet? Or would you prefer champagne—there's always some on ice.'

'No, thanks. I'll have a Campari.' She saw him smile. 'What's so funny?'

'Your choice of drink. It's a rather sharp one.' He poured out a measure. 'It reflects your usual mood with me!'

Taking the glass from him, she turned away. Sharp with him? Well, yes, she supposed she was. Until a few days ago she had found it difficult even to be civil to him. She sipped her drink, wishing he didn't make her feel so gauche.

Surreptitiously she studied him. He had resumed his seat by the fireplace, and a nearby lamp—shining down on his head—gave a silvery sheen to his fawn-coloured hair. Oblivious of her regard, he was cleaning his glasses with a handkerchief, the movement slow and deliberate. Then he tilted his head and looked in her direction.

Without spectacles he appeared strangely vulnerable, innocent almost. It surprised her, as did the length of his lashes—a darker fawn than his hair, and thick and spiky as a child's. But the fine lines radiating from the corners of his eyes were anything but a child's, speaking of strain and long hours of working.

'This is the first time I've seen you without your glasses,' she said.

'You have the advantage over me, then.'

'Meaning?'

'I can't see *myself* without them!'

A quick movement of his hand replaced them and once again he was the inscrutable man she knew him to be. Just as well, she thought irritably. If he started looking half-way human she might begin to think he was!

Before dinner he certainly made an effort to appear it, and was so unusually talkative she was afraid he'd grow personal. Deliberately she steered the conversation to his work, pleased when he took the bait and started regaling her with facts about the new drugs they were manufacturing, and the research they were doing.

'I've no objection to spending money if I can be certain of a decent profit at the end,' he explained. 'But with the government dictating our price-structure, it's a whole new ball game. They forget one has to answer to shareholders.'

'My father's the biggest,' Sandra said, 'and he'll go along with anything you suggest.'

'Would *you*? Your trust fund has the same size holding.'

'I don't interfere in its management,' she replied. 'I suppose you think that's empty-headed of me?'

'Not at all. Your interests are artistic, not commercial.' He paused momentarily. 'I think you're wasting your talent at Causten's, though. You should aim higher.'

It was a back-handed compliment—typical of him—and her growing liking for him vanished.

'Sorry,' he said softly. 'I didn't realise my remark could be taken two ways.'

His apology did not appease her, and it was a relief when Thomas announced that dinner was served. They chatted desultorily during the meal, and when they returned to the drawing-room for coffee Sandra settled herself as far from Randall as she could without having to shout, irritated when he came and sat next to her on the sofa.

'You know your father isn't getting any better, Sandra.'

His words were like a bolt from the blue, the matter-of-fact way he said them doing nothing to ease the shock.

'No, I didn't. I thought he was on the mend.'

'I'm afraid not. I spoke to the specialist this morning and he says there's been severe damage to the heart.'

'Why didn't Dr Baxter tell *me*?' she asked indignantly. 'I only saw him this afternoon.'

'Your father doesn't want you to know. However, I thought you should.'

The cup in Sandra's hand rattled, and she set it down untouched. 'I'm glad you told me, Randall. I'm not a child who has to be protected from the truth.'

'I agree. But please don't let your father know I've told you.'

She blinked rapidly, determined not to let Randall see her cry. 'I think we should go see him,' she murmured, moving to the door. 'He'll get restless otherwise.'

'Not if he thinks we're talking amicably!'

She sniffed. 'I keep forgetting how well you know him.'

Randall followed her up the stairs. 'Well enough to know we should at least pretend friendship. It will distress him if we behave like enemies.'

'We aren't enemies, Randall, but I won't have you giving him the impression we might marry.'

Randall's stride did not falter. 'All I've done is assure him I'll take care of you if anything happens to him.'

'You mean take care of my shares,' she shot back. 'That's all you're concerned with.'

'Your continual harping on my financial interest in you is becoming a bore. I suggest we drop it.'

'I will—if you do me the favour of dropping *me*.'

'I couldn't marry you anyway,' he murmured. 'If manners indicate age, you're still a ten-year-old!'

Not trusting herself to reply, Sandra flung open her father's door, remembering—just in time—to put a smile on her face as she marched into the room.

In bed that night, Sandra wryly admitted that Randall's unfailing ability to make her feel stupid was his most aggravating characteristic. No matter how hard she tried to be cool, he always aroused her to a display of infantile temper.

Well, from now on she would amaze him with her politeness and astound him with her worldliness! Amused by the idea of being able to astound Randall, she drifted off to sleep.

She awoke next morning from a disturbing dream about Barry, and the uneasy feeling it engendered made her decide to go to see him. If she left here by ten, she could be at Causten's in time for him to take her to lunch—if he were free. If he weren't she would spend the night with him, which was probably the best way of erasing his doubts and showing him she loved him.

'There's no need for you to rush back,' her father assured her when she told him she had some work to finish for the agency and might have to stay overnight. 'See some of your friends while you're there. In fact, why not invite a few for the weekend?'

'I may ask Barry,' she said carefully.

'You promised not to rush into anything with him,' Edward Harris reminded her.

'I know. And I won't. So stop worrying I'll elope!' Kissing him goodbye, she hurried out before he could ask any further questions.

There was little traffic on the roads and she reached London before noon. Parking her car in Causten's basement garage, she charged up to Barry's office, disconcerted to find it empty. More than that—pristine; a sign he hadn't set foot in it! Frowning, she went to ask his secretary where he was.

'Working from home,' the girl informed her. 'He asked me not to tell anyone because he doesn't want any interruptions. But I'm sure he didn't mean you!'

Smiling her thanks, Sandra set off for Knightsbridge. She was pleased not to be seeing Barry at the office, for it was easier to say what she wanted in the intimacy of his home. Of course being there had its own danger— he might want her to prove there and then that she meant what she said, and her pulses hammered with fear. But it was a fear she had to overcome.

Trembling, she drew up outside his mews house and rang the bell. There was no answer, and she was about to ring again when the door opened and he stood there in pyjamas and dressing-gown, gaping at her.

'Sandra! What on earth are you doing here?'

'Visiting you!' She stepped past him into the hall, her smile freezing as a pretty brunette emerged from the kitchen in one of Barry's shirts, clearly revealing that she wore nothing underneath.

Blindly Sandra swung back to the front door, but Barry barred her way.

'Wait! If I'd known you were coming I'd——'

'—have baked a cake? Don't bother apologising, Barry. I'm the one who's sorry—for barging in on you like this.' From the corner of her eye she saw the girl retreat into the kitchen and close the door.

'Don't make a mountain out of a molehill!' Barry gripped her elbow and propelled her into the living-room. 'You know damn well I love you.'

'You've a funny way of showing it!'

'Jane means nothing to me.'

'That I can believe!' she retorted. 'No girl means anything to you.'

'*You* did. And when you rejected me... Hell, you didn't expect me to enter a monastery!'

'If you genuinely cared for me you wouldn't be able to make love to anyone else.'

'It wasn't making love,' he retorted. 'It was sex. Don't you know the difference?'

It was the cruellest question he could have thrown at her, and she shuddered. 'Darn right I know the difference! You're the one who doesn't!' Pushing him violently aside, she ran out to her car.

She must have been blind not to have seen him for the womaniser he was. Was she doomed to go on making mistakes about the men she met, as naïve today as she had been all those years ago?

It was a dismal thought, and she considered it soberly as she returned to her apartment and packed her clothes. London had no more to offer her, and she would return to her father, the one man she could trust. She'd never let herself fall in love again. All a man did was use you. Barry regarded her as a sex object and Randall as a means of securing his position.

She was carrying her cases into the hall when the entryphone rang. It could only be Barry, and for a split second she debated whether to ignore it. Then reason won and she answered it, amazed how calmly she could speak.

'Go away, Barry. I don't want to see you.'

'We can't part like this. You've got to let me explain.'

And hear more glib assurances that weren't worth the breath that expelled them? As she went to hang up, pride stopped her. Why give him the satisfaction of knowing how deeply he had hurt her? Why not pretend her anger had come from pique, not love? At least it would stop him boasting he could once have married the heiress to the Harris millions!

'OK, come on up,' she said laconically.

Taking the stairs two at a time, he did, looking anything but the well groomed man she knew. He must have slipped on the first clothes that came to hand, and hadn't stopped to shave either, for blue stubble still darkened his chin.

'I know how badly you feel,' he began, 'but Jane means nothing to me—I swear it.'

'I believe you.'

'Then how come you ran off?'

'Because the moment I saw you with her, I realised I didn't love you.'

'Don't give me that! You were furious with me.'

'Only because you hurt my *pride*.' Sandra forced herself to speak calmly. 'But now I've had a chance to cool down, I feel nothing. No anger, no pain. Just relief that I found out in time.'

'You're lying,' he said bluntly. 'You're only saying it to hurt me. Not that I blame you; in your shoes I'd do the same. But for God's sake don't ruin our future because I was a fool! I love you, Sandra, and when you said you'd never live with me unless I married you, I was so angry I wanted to hurt you. Not very creditable, I know, but don't make me pay for it with the rest of my life!'

He had made out such a good case for himself that Sandra almost forgave him. Almost, but not quite. In his way he probably did love her, but his way could never be hers. She'd always doubt his fidelity, be jealous of every girl he worked with, worry if he went on a business trip. Hard though it was to walk away from him, it would be harder if she stayed.

'I'm sorry, Barry, but it's still no.'

Expecting another plea, she was unprepared for the unpleasant change that came over him. The eyes narrowed malevolently and the full mouth thinned to a bitter line, the words emanating from it vicious and ugly.

'If you can fall out of love so fast, you're no better than what you accused *me* of being! You only wanted me because you thought I was hard to get.'

'There's no need to hold an inquest.' Sandra prayed for him to go. If they went on talking, she'd give herself away by bursting into tears. 'I made a mistake about you, and I like to put my mistakes behind me!'

'I bet you do,' sneered Barry. 'Did living among the rich again make you decide to marry the man Daddy wants for you? That's the real reason you're walking out on me, isn't it?'

She let a shrug speak for her, and had the pleasure of seeing him redden with anger.

'Who is he?' he demanded. 'A Norfolk yokel with straw in his hair and a fortune in the bank?'

'A man I can respect as well as love,' she corrected coolly. 'That's so important, don't you think?'

Without a word, Barry swung round on his heel and stormed out, leaving Sandra to sink into a chair. The ugly scene had taken its toll of her, though it had bolstered her pride—and given Barry's a hell of a jolt! How livid he had been when she had described her mythical new love as someone she could respect! Yet she had made herself a blueprint of the man with whom she would like to share her life: someone whose integrity she would never doubt, whose faithfulness she could take on trust. In short, a man of honour.

The gloom of late afternoon had settled a misty blue haze around Wideacres as Sandra walked into her father's room.

'I thought you were staying over,' he said.

'I missed you too much.'

'Twaddle!' But he looked pleased. 'Saw this Barry fellow, did you?'

'Yes.'

'When's he coming down?'

'He isn't.' Sandra dug her hands into the pockets of her dress. 'I think I must be fickle, Dad. Seeing him again made me realise I didn't care for him as much as I'd thought.'

'That's not fickle—it's sensible! Never did like the sound of him. But won't it be awkward having to work with him?'

'I'm not going to. I'm staying here with you.'

'No need for that,' came the gruff answer. 'You've your own life to lead.'

'I fancy leading it here for a while.' She perched on the side of the bed. 'Do anything interesting today?'

'Looked at some old photo albums. Brought back memories too,' he sighed. 'Made me realise that everything I've built up will soon fall into strange hands.'

Sandra's heart lurched, but she managed to speak casually. 'Randall isn't a stranger, darling. You've always said you regard him as family.'

'I know. But when it comes to the crunch, he isn't. No one of my flesh and blood will have a real say in the running of the company.'

'I'll still be a major shareholder,' Sandra reminded him and, eager to change the subject, launched into a fictitious account of her day. She was in the middle of it when Randall walked in, his briefcase indicating he had come directly from the office.

'If I'd realised you were going to town,' he said to her after greeting her father, 'I'd have given you a lift.'

Thank goodness he hadn't! The strain of driving for several hours alone with him was too awful to contemplate!

'I'll tell you next time,' she lied urbanely, and seeing the pleasure on her father's face, knew he had read more into her polite platitude than he should.

'Stay to dinner, Randall,' she heard him say. 'Sandra will enjoy your company.'

'Randall may have other plans,' she put in quickly.

'Let him speak for himself!'

'I'd like to stay,' came the reply. 'But I'll go home and change first.'

'Why bother?' she asked rudely. 'One dark suit's like another!'

He laughed. It was a rare sound and she couldn't help liking it. Soft yet deep, it was nothing like his voice, which was always colourless.

'I'll have to prove you wrong, Sandra,' he was saying. 'I'll be back at eight with a new image!'

'You've put him on his mettle,' her father chuckled when Randall had left. 'You'd better wear something special too!'

It wasn't much fun dressing for a man who excited her as much as warmed-up potato, but she had no choice, and put on a gold silk Kenzo that deepened the colour of her tawny eyes.

'You look just like your mother,' Edward Harris said gruffly when she came in to show herself off, knowing it would please him.

'I've got your nose,' she teased.

'As well as my obstinacy! Come closer and let me have a good look at you.'

She did, and bent to kiss him. Her perfume wafted around him, a delicate fragrance reminiscent of freesias. She felt beautiful, the silk jersey dress swathing itself round her small, full breasts and rounded hips, before falling in fluid lines to the floor. To complement it, she had set her hair into a mass of curls, and tiny fronds, catching the light, made it appear more silver than gold.

'You should be married with children,' her father muttered. 'Time I was a grandfather!'

'I'll oblige when I find the right man.'

'Randall——'

'No!'

'Why not? He loves you very much. Look how long he's waited for you, and never so much as glanced at another woman.'

'How do you know?'

'If there was someone else, he'd have told me.'

Surprisingly, Sandra found it easy to imagine women finding Randall attractive. Remembering his passionate kiss the night he had asked her to marry him, she knew his cool manner hid fire. The memory brought a rush of colour to her cheeks, and her father, misinterpreting it, looked pleased.

A car door slammed and she went to the door. 'That must be Randall now. I'd better go down.'

'Let him come up. We can all have a drink together.'

'Oh no, we can't! You rest. We'll be in to see you later.'

'Yes, Miss Bossy Boots.'

Grinning, she went out.

CHAPTER FIVE

SURPRISED by her nervousness, Sandra sped down to the drawing-room.

Randall had promised her a new image, and oh boy, had he kept his word! In place of a conventional dinner-jacket, he wore finest black suede, with a pleated white shirt and maroon bow tie and cummerbund. His hair, normally sleek to his head, was left casual, giving him a younger look. He had even changed his glasses, the heavy tortoiseshell rims replaced by narrow gold ones, the top curve of the metal so fine it merged into the curving arc of his eyebrows, and though the eyes themselves were still masked by the lenses, the whole effect was less intimidating.

'Will I pass?' he asked.

'Why—er—yes. It's a great improvement. You don't look half so stiff and stuffy.'

'You mean Pearson the Paragon's become Pearson the Playboy?'

'*Are* you?' she asked mischievously.

'Mind if I take the Fifth Amendment?'

She shrugged and went to the drinks tray. 'What will you have?'

'I think your appearance calls for champagne. You're looking especially stunning.' He lifted a bottle from the silver ice bucket and carefully eased out the cork.

'It hasn't popped!' she exclaimed.

'It doesn't if it's opened properly. If the air bubbles are released in an explosion, it leaves less in the wine itself.'

She giggled, and his head tilted.

'Have I missed out on the joke?'

'It's you. You may have changed your looks, but you're as pedantic as ever!'

'Didn't you find the explanation interesting, then?'

'Actually, it was. But I didn't really want one. Not everything I say requires an answer.'

'I'll remember that.' He handed her a tall, fluted glass, his rare smile allowing her a glimpse of even white teeth.

'Cheers,' he said.

'What a boring toast. Can't you do better?'

'Much better. But I didn't want to embarrass you. However...' He raised his glass higher. 'To Sandra, whose sparkle makes Dom Perignon seem flat, whose honey-gold hair dulls the sun, whose lips——'

'OK, you've proved your point,' she cut in hastily.

'And made you blush too. I'm surprised. I thought you'd be used to compliments.'

'Snappier ones.'

'They'd certainly match your mood!'

There was no mistaking his irony, and though she knew she had been rude, she could not bring herself to apologise. Instead she seated herself in a chair by the window, with none near it he could occupy.

'I didn't expect you back from London so soon,' he went on conversationally. 'Your father said you were staying over.'

'I changed my mind.'

'Does that include the boyfriend?'

'What's that supposed to mean?' demanded Sandra.

'That I believe you have a special one.'

'Lots of special ones, Randall. A girl as sparkling as champagne would hardly be content with one!'

'*You* would. I think you're still waiting for Mr Right to come along on a white charger and carry you off!'

'To set the record straight, until today, I thought I'd found him!'

'What happened?'

'Another girl.'

'Would it sound trite if I offered a shoulder and a willing ear?' Randall asked.

'Not only trite, but trying too hard. You can't win me by offering me champagne and sympathy!'

'There was no ulterior motive in my offer. Merely a genuine wish to help.'

He looked as if he meant it, which made her doubly irritated. While he remained the *bête noire* of her existence she could cope with him. As Mr Nice Guy she was at a loss.

'Thanks, Randall, but I've enough friends without needing *your* shoulder to cry on.'

He regarded her blandly, though the small vein pulsing at his temple showed his anger. If only he'd give vent to it instead of maintaining his icy calm.

'You enjoy provoking me, don't you?' he said.

'Can one provoke a stone?'

'You're being childish.'

'I'd hardly call you the epitome of sophistication.' She was incensed by his patronising tone. 'All you're interested in are test tubes and profits.'

'Not *quite* all,' he countered. 'Though I won't deny a certain single-mindedness.'

'Particularly where I'm concerned. Can't you damn well take no for an answer?'

Randall's mouth thinned. 'I know your father's illness has put you under a strain, but I *won't* be your whipping-boy for ever. Even *my* patience can wear thin.'

'I can't wait for the day,' she said sweetly. 'It would at least show you're capable of real feeling.'

His head lifted sharply, his lenses glittering as they caught the light of a nearby lamp. 'If you need proof that I'm human, I'm more than willing to oblige.'

With an immense effort she stared back at him, knowing she had walked into a trap of her own making and refusing to let him intimidate her.

'I'll take your word for it, Randall.'

'As you wish.' With a sardonic smile he took her glass from her hand and went to refill it.

They drank in a silence that remained unbroken until Thomas came in to say dinner was served. Two places had been set at one end of the long, mahogany dining-table; the rich wood glowed warmly in the light of the gently flickering candles in the Georgian silver candle-sticks, lending a romantic air to the otherwise austere room.

What a boring evening this is going to be, Sandra thought, picking up her fork, and was all set for the silence to continue when Randall broke it by asking her about the work she did at Causten's. Cunning swine! He thought he'd hold her interest that way. And of course he did, for his questions were interesting, and the comments he gave to her monosyllabic answers showed an unexpected knowledge of how an advertising agency was run.

'I thought you were only interested in chemistry and making money,' she said after he had made a particularly insightful comment.

'I'm also interested in how we spend it, and since our advertising costs run into millions, I've made it my business to know where the money goes.'

'You like putting your finger in everyone's pie, don't you?'

'That's the job of a Managing Director.' He paused while duck and wild rice was served. 'Putting my finger in *your* pie,' he went on with dry humour, 'what are your plans for the future?'

'Nothing, beyond staying here as long as I'm needed.'

'Won't you be bored away from your friends and work?'

'I was born and brought up here,' she replied. 'I'm used to the quiet life.'

'Yet you couldn't wait to leave it.'

'Only because I wanted to establish my independence.'

'And now you have, you're ready to return to the fold?'

'I came back to be with my father,' she explained.

'Not because a man let you down?'

'What the hell business is it of yours?' she came at him.

'A great deal,' Randall said blandly. 'I once asked you to marry me.'

'This is a recorded message!' she flung at him.

'And one I won't erase. In fact I planned to repeat it over coffee—not during dinner.'

'Afraid it would give me indigestion?'

'No. Nor did I think I had to get you drunk to obtain a civil answer!'

At last he was showing anger, his pale grey eyes glinting like chips of ice. Delighted she had finally pierced his smugness, Sandra set down her knife and fork. 'Is "No, thank you, Randall dear," civil enough?'

'At least it's a basis to work from!'

She glared at him. Either he was trying to rile her or he was thick-skinned as a rhinoceros. Didn't he understand a point-blank refusal when he heard one?

'You're impossible!' she snapped. 'Give me one good reason why I should say yes.'

'How about two?' All trace of his anger was gone. 'Affection and stability.'

Flummoxed, she leaned back in her chair. 'How can you feel any affection for me when all I've ever done is insult you?'

The smile that lit his face was unexpected, softening his austere features. 'You're forgetting I've watched you grow from a cocky teenager into a lovely young woman; from a gosling into a swan.'

'But I've never even been nice to you!'

'In the beginning you were.'

'From fifteen to seventeen? Come off it, Randall! You wouldn't still be carrying a torch for me if I weren't my father's daughter.'

'How convinced you are that you know my feelings.' His head tilted. 'What would you say if I told you I loved you?'

If! At least he found it hard to lie outright. Yet she would have respected him more if he had abandoned pretence completely and put his proposal on a business footing.

'It won't work, Randall. We've nothing in common.'

'A marriage based on friendship has as much chance of succeeding as one based on so-called "love"—which is generally nothing more than sexual attraction.'

Sandra tried picturing being married to him: no highs, no lows, no quarrels, no passion. How boring! But at least he'd be dependable, which was more than could be said for Barry.

'It's still no,' she said. 'I can't marry someone I don't love.'

'Our marriage could be platonic to start with,' he responded smoothly.

'To end with, too! I could never be a real wife to you.'

'I think you could, given time; and I'm prepared to back my instincts.'

His confidence annoyed her. How sure of himself he was!

'Your instincts may be great in business,' she said, 'but you're dealing with a woman now, Randall, not a company take-over!'

'The same tactics apply, though. Persistence, patience and knowing when it's the right time to strike!'

His certainty unnerved her, and her eyes went to the long, supple fingers clasping his wine glass, nails rounded and well manicured, skin smooth as velvet. On his wrist was a slim band of crocodile encasing a wafer of gold: unobtrusive, perfect, but lifeless as the man himself. One flaw only, and he'd have been more real, more exciting perhaps—like Barry. Yet how shallow Barry's so-called attributes were compared with the values she held dear.

A knock at the door made them both turn. It was the nurse, and Sandra's heart thumped.

'Daddy! Is——'

'He's fine,' the woman said quickly. 'But he'd like to see you and Mr Pearson before I settle him for the night.'

Dropping her napkin on the table, Sandra hurried out, Randall hard on her heels. She might not like the man, but she could not deny his fondness for her father. At one stage she had assumed he was putting on an act—but when his attitude remained unchanged even as his power in the company grew, she had accepted it as genuine. Probably the only genuine emotion he was capable of!

'Didn't mean to interrupt your dinner,' Edward Harris said as they came in, 'but the nurse insists on bedding me down like a potted plant, and I wanted to say goodnight to you first.'

Sandra sensed there was more to his summons than this. 'Anything bothering you, Daddy?'

'Nothing, girlie.'

The endearment, rarely used, brought tears to her eyes, and she blinked rapidly to stop them falling.

'I was thinking of all the things I haven't said,' he went on gruffly, 'and it made me restless.'

'It isn't always necessary to put feelings into words,' she murmured. 'If you love someone, they can tell.'

Edward Harris turned towards Randall. 'You *will* take care of her, won't you? She thinks she's a grown woman, but she's still a child.'

'Not so much a child that I can't be Randall's wife!'

Incredulously Sandra heard herself speak. Had she gone mad? What in heaven's name had come over her? Her father's radiant expression was her answer. She wanted to put his mind at rest, to make him believe she would be taken care of when he was gone. Yet there was more to it than that. In a word—Barry. She had told him there was another man in her life, and now she was proving it! No 'Norfolk yokel with straw in his hair,' as he had so rudely said, but a high-flying model for British industry! What a shock Barry would have when he read it in the papers!

'I'm delighted, delighted.' Edward Harris was beaming from ear to ear. 'How did you get her to change her mind, Randall? You didn't concoct this to please me, did you? I may be sick but I'm not senile, and I don't want any lies.'

'It's the truth,' said Randall, placing an arm across Sandra's shoulder. 'The main reason for my persistence was that it's the only way I can get to call you "Father"!'

Edward Harris chuckled. 'I'd like "Grandfather" even more! You two have given me the best incentive to get well again. But don't wait for me to walk up the aisle with you, Sandra. That could take a while.'

'We're in no hurry,' she said quickly.

'Nonsense! Young people are always in a hurry. Old ones too, if I'm anything to go by! I can't wait to see you married. How about a month from now?'

Sandra was wondering how to stall, when Randall spoke.

'Actually I was thinking in terms of next week.'

'That's far too soon!' Sandra whirled on him. She had only been thinking of an engagement, and Randall was clever enough to know it. 'It's fun being engaged,' she added with a girlish little laugh. 'Let's enjoy it for a while.'

'We'll enjoy marriage more,' Randall said smoothly. 'Besides, I want to take you with me to the States.'

'The States?'

'That's why I'm rushing you, darling. I have to go there on business, and as I'll be away at least a month, I thought we'd combine it with a honeymoon.'

Trust Randall to think of combining business with a honeymoon!

'We haven't called the banns yet,' she stated, trying to hide her triumph at circumventing him.

'You can have a church wedding later,' her father put in, 'when I'll be able to attend.'

'My sentiments entirely,' Randall added, and Sandra, glancing from one man to the other, felt her life was being taken over.

Paradoxically, knowing her immediate future was settled brought her a strange sense of peace. That she didn't love Randall, that she was only marrying him from filial duty seemed unimportant at this juncture. Disillusioned by Barry, she could not envisage finding true love with anyone else; and this being the case, perhaps it wasn't so foolish to settle for the even tenor of a sterile marriage! Or was it?

In the middle of the night Sandra awoke in a cold sweat. What had she let herself in for? Better to remain a spinster the rest of her life than marry Randall! It was a recipe for disaster, and first thing in the morning she would tell him.

Eight o'clock found her pacing the library, dressed, and awash with black coffee which, far from steadying her nerves, had exacerbated them. Waiting round was no help either, but she couldn't face talking to him in the intimacy of his home, and had to contain her impatience until he arrived at the office.

At eight-thirty she could wait no longer, and was crossing the hall when she saw Thomas running down the stairs towards her. One look at his face sent her dashing up to her father, where she found the nurse giving him an injection.

'Just a little spasm,' the woman said composedly, though her eyes spoke another story, and Sandra kissed her freedom goodbye.

'Where are you off to so early?' Edward Harris asked faintly.

'What a question to ask a bride-to-be! Shopping, of course.'

'Then don't let me stop you. I feel fine now.'

Knowing better than to argue, Sandra kissed him gently and went downstairs. Fate was obviously on Randall's side, and she had better accept that fact and make the best of it.

She reminded herself of this later that morning when he unexpectedly arrived at the house.

'I've brought some papers for your father to sign,' he explained. 'But I've just spoken to the nurse and left them with her.'

'I don't want him bothered with anything,' Sandra said belligerently.

'I agree. But it will mean his having to give *you* power of attorney, and that might distress him more. Let's wait a few days and see how things go.' Randall eyed her. 'You're looking pale as a ghost.'

'I hardly slept last night.' She paused, then said in a rush, 'If there hadn't been this emergency, I'd have been on my way to tell you I can't marry you.'

'I rather thought you might.'

'But now I'm stuck with you!'

'It might turn out better than you think,' he suggested.

'It will be a disaster!' she said emphatically.

'Or a resounding success. Why not wait and see?'

'Will nothing dent your arrogant belief that you know me better than I know myself?' she stormed.

'Confident belief, Sandra, not arrogant. Confident enough to believe that one day our marriage will be for real.'

'Never, never!'

'That's a word I won't accept. I'm thirty-four and don't intend being in a bath-chair when my son asks me to play cricket with him.'

Sandra caught her breath. It was hard enough thinking of Randall as her husband, but as father of her children...

'It's impossible!' she cried.

'Then I'll leave it to you to tell your father—because I won't.'

But that was impossible too, and Randall knew it. Mutinously Sandra watched him take off his glasses and polish them, a habit of his when pondering what to say. The blue-white lids were lowered and she wondered what colour grey his irises were now—pale with anger or dark with determination?—and was given her answer when he raised his head and smoky grey eyes stared myopically at her.

'Don't be pessimistic about our future, Sandra. You might find me a good lover.'

'I'm looking for more than technical expertise,' she snapped. 'I don't want to go to bed with you and I never will!'

'Do you find me repulsive, then?'

His question startled her, and almost without realising it she made a physical inventory of him, accepting again that some women would admire the tall, lean figure, the pale, precise features and silvery beige hair.

'I'm waiting for your answer,' he said softly, and she shrugged and half turned away.

'I don't find you repulsive, Randall, merely a turn-off.'

'Why?'

'Because you make me feel naïve.'

'Considering the people you mixed with in London, I hardly think "naïve" applicable!'

'Oh, you...!'

She was at a loss for words, and he filled the silence with his own.

'It doesn't give me any pleasure to know how much you dislike me. If it weren't for your father's condition, I'd be happy not to set eyes on you again.'

'You change your mind pretty quick, don't you? A moment ago you said——'

'I know,' he cut across her, 'and I was wrong. I see now that you aren't ready for marriage. Your sophistication is skin-deep, Sandra. Underneath, you're an immature girl afraid to love. You've a lot of growing up to do, and it's my misfortune to be stuck with you.'

Had a moth bitten her, she could not have been more astonished. Talk about a worm turning! Not that Randall was a worm, she amended hastily. But till now he'd always ignored her insults, and to have him lambast her was as surprising as it was unpleasant. But she'd never let him know it. If he cut her to ribbons with his tongue, she'd wipe away the blood and say it was red ink!

'Then I take it our marriage will be platonic?' she questioned coolly.

'You can take nothing of the sort!' Although he didn't raise his voice, there was steel in it. 'As I said before, I want children.'

'With another wife, then, not with me. The moment I can, I'll get free of you.'

'I hope that won't be for many years,' he answered softly. 'And as a loving daughter, I'm sure you do too.'

How cleverly he knew where to hit her, and how little compunction he had in doing it! Without answering him, Sandra stalked out.

Exhausted by their confrontation and her sleepless night, she went to lie down. She should be furious with Randall, yet she was too numb to feel anything, and she closed her eyes and let her mind drift.

She was awakened by the nurse gently tapping her shoulder. 'What's wrong?' she asked groggily.

'Nothing. But Mr Harris would like you to have tea with him.'

'Tea? I haven't had lunch yet!'

'It's gone four,' the nurse smiled. 'But you were so sound asleep we didn't like to wake you.'

'Gone four? Good heavens!' Sandra sat up, yawning. 'Give me a minute to come to myself, and I'll be along.'

She found her father cheerful and apologetic for the fright he had given her that morning.

'The nurse shouldn't call you every time I get one of these little spasms. It alarms you for nothing.' He helped himself to an almond biscuit. 'Hmm, good. Which reminds me, it's time we discussed your wedding reception. After dinner tonight, why don't you and Randall join me here?'

'I'm not sure if he's coming over,' she said. Indeed, remembering the way they had parted, she wasn't even certain she'd see him before the wedding!

'Of course he'll be here,' came the testy reply. 'He left word with the nurse.'

The prospect of another confrontation with Randall set Sandra's nerves jangling, and her longing to be with Barry was so strong that she made some excuse and left the room.

In her own room she paced the floor like a caged animal, tears of frustration pouring down her cheeks as she relived the past few days and wished she could turn back the clock. If only she hadn't gone to Barry's house uninvited and seen that damned girl! Yet for how long would her ignorance have remained bliss? Sooner or later she was bound to have discovered his true character.

The chiming of a downstairs clock sent her dashing into the bathroom, where icy water decreased the puffiness of her lids, and skilful make-up restored her to a semblance of normality. Then she donned an understated dress in muted shades of blue and green, braided her hair into a coronet and, with a circlet of pearls around her neck, presented the perfect image of a Yuppie wife-to-be!

Randall arrived at eight—prompt as always—but looking so unexpectedly tired that her determination to remain aloof vanished, and she instantly poured him a whisky and put it in his hand.

'You look as if you've had a tough day,' she commented.

Nodding, he sank into a chair. 'Two long meetings and a couple of hours' shopping in between.'

'You should have skipped tonight.'

'I wanted to give you this.' Rising, he took a little black velvet box from his pocket and handed it to her.

It was a repetition of another time—four years ago—and strangely reluctant to open it, she lifted the lid. On a cushion of satin lay a square-cut sapphire ring, the deep blue stone surrounded by heart-shaped diamonds.

It was clearly antique and extremely valuable, totally unlike anything Barry—whose taste ran to the modern—would have bought her. Yet it was exactly to her taste, though she would have died rather than admit it to the man in front of her.

'I didn't know if you'd have preferred something modern,' he murmured.

'You could have asked me!'

'I thought I'd take a chance.'

And had proved himself accurate. Did he never put a foot wrong!

'It'll do,' she shrugged. 'Where did you get it?'

'Sotheby's, today.'

No wonder he was so tired. He had dashed up to London for their sale.

Randall took the ring from the box and unceremoniously slipped it on to her finger. 'Good. It fits perfectly.'

'Let's go and show it to Daddy,' she said quickly.

'Not so fast.' With a swift movement he pulled her into his arms and pressed his mouth upon hers.

Like a statue she accepted his touch, determined to remain unresponsive. But his lips were subtle and caressing, and his hand, moving lightly across her back, sent a shiver across her skin. Abruptly he let go of her and went to the door.

Bemused, she followed him, irritated that he could so easily master his emotions. But who was she kidding? His emotions weren't involved. It was all part of the act he insisted on playing.

'It's a beautiful ring,' Edward Harris said when he saw it. 'I've been lying here thinking of the reception, and wondering if we should put a marquee in the garden.'

'I think not,' Randall said, giving Sandra a sidelong glance. 'We'd both prefer keeping the celebration to a few close friends and relatives. That way we can catch an early flight to New York, and arrive there at a reasonable hour. Right, darling?'

Feeling like a lamb being led to the slaughter, Sandra resisted the urge to say 'Baa!' and nodded.

'You're only keeping it small because of me,' Mr Harris grunted. 'Wish I weren't such an old crock!'

'As long as you're well enough to be with us,' Sandra said huskily, 'I don't care if you're the *only* guest.'

The next few days sped by. Despite thinking sackcloth and ashes more appropriate for her wedding dress, Sandra dutifully went to London and bought a cream silk Zandra Rhodes.

She had deliberately not invited any of her friends—she didn't want them celebrating a marriage that held no meaning for her—and, walking down Bond Street in search of cream kid sandals, she was deeply depressed that what should have been the most joyous occasion of her life was only heralding a term of imprisonment.

How long would it last once her father... Angrily she pushed away the thought. How could she think of his death as her own road to freedom? Yet it was difficult not to, and because she prided herself on her ability to call a spade a spade—she was not Edward Harris's daughter for nothing—she faced the fact that when he did eventually go, she would no longer be tied to a loveless union.

Amazing that Randall didn't realise this! Or maybe he was hoping to wear down her resistance before then.

'Never!' she said aloud, and saw a passer-by fling her an odd look.

Pink-cheeked, she dashed into Rayne's, found the shoes she wanted, and was emerging with the parcel when she saw the petite figure of Linda Maynard, an erstwhile colleague from Causten's.

'Hi, stranger!' Linda hugged her. 'Sorry to hear about your father. Barry told me he was ill.'

'Then you know we——'

'Parted, and you turned out to be a millionairess with a gold-plated bath? Yes, I know it all, and I promise it won't make any difference to my devoted friendship.'

Sandra laughed, knowing it to be true, for Linda couldn't care less about money. 'I suppose you also saw my engagement in the papers?'

'You bet! Can you spare time for lunch and a gossip?'

'An hour only. I don't want to drive back in the rush hour.'

'I'm so glad you broke with Barry,' Linda ventured as they munched quiche in a wine bar some ten minutes later. 'Beats me how you ever fell for him. Heck! I shouldn't have said that. Sorry.'

'Forget it. You're right anyway.'

'Thank goodness you realise it. Barry may be set for the top in the advertising world, but as a human being he's the pits.'

Sandra was taken aback by the girl's criticism, and wished her friend had been more forthcoming months ago. Yet it wouldn't have done any good. She would still have been deaf to the truth.

'Sorry I can't ask you to the wedding,' she apologised as they rose to leave. 'But it's a very quiet one. I'll call you when I get back from honeymoon.'

'There'll be no hard feelings if you don't. I'm not part of your world any more, Sandra.'

'I don't choose my friends by their bank balance,' Sandra snorted, but on her way home she pondered over Linda's remark. Maybe the super-rich could never be on genuinely easy terms with those who weren't. It was a disheartening thought, for it went against all her beliefs, and later that evening she found herself mentioning it to Randall. She didn't quite know why she was confiding in him—probably because he was there and had a listening ear.

'Your friend sounds sensible,' he commented, sipping his brandy and regarding her enigmatically. 'Like it or not, money does create barriers.'

'Are all *your* friends rich?'

He smiled. 'That's the first personal question you've asked me! I hope it won't be the last.'

'Why should I *have* to ask? You should be more forthcoming.'

'You've never given the impression of being interested.'

On the verge of saying she wasn't, Sandra stopped. She had vowed to be dignified, and would be so if it killed her!

'As I'll be playing the part of your wife,' she responded lightly, 'I should at least have an idea of your background.'

'I'll give you my curriculum vitae.'

'Thanks.'

'When you've played the part long enough,' he added, 'you may find it fits like a second skin.'

'Or a hair shirt!' The retort escaped before she could stop it, and he chuckled.

'I'd be lost if you stopped disliking me, Sandra. You're like a flea to a dog!'

She chuckled too. It was the first humorous exchange they had shared, and instinctively she knew it wouldn't be the last. Perhaps it was for the best. They would be linked together for the foreseeable future, and it would be less wearing on her nerves if they were friends rather than enemies.

From beneath her lashes she watched him sip his brandy. Randall an enemy? That was going a bit far. 'A business husband' was a much better description; added to which it made her feel better to see their marriage as a contract for a limited period only.

CHAPTER SIX

IT WAS a calm, cool-headed Sandra—though inwardly a
trembling one—who became Mrs Randall Pearson the
following Saturday. She was glad her father hadn't been
allowed to attend the ceremony. It was enough of a farce
without his adding to it by his delighted belief that all
his hopes for her had come true!

Resentfully she slanted her eyes at Randall. He was
the epitome of a self-satisfied, self-contained man. A
faint smile curved his mouth, and his cheeks were tinged
pink as the roses that perfumed the room. There must
have been ten dozen of them: magnificent blooms that
lent an air of festivity to a room normally drab and of-
ficious. Unaccountably Sandra felt a stirring of pity for
him. He was doing his best to make this seem a real
wedding, while all she was doing was wishing it wasn't
taking place!

She looked from him to the smiling faces of two of
her father's oldest friends and their wives, their wit-
nesses. They'd have a fit if they knew what a reluctant
bride she was! Reluctant? That was putting it mildly!
She was furiously, ragingly trapped!

Was there ever a bride who had dressed with less regard
to her appearance? Who actually resented knowing she
looked beautiful?

With a start she became aware that Randall was
slipping a narrow platinum ring on her finger.

'Put yours on me,' he commanded softly, handing her
an identical one to slip on his finger.

Nervously she obeyed him. 'I didn't think you'd wear
one,' she whispered.

71

'It binds us together.'

His eyes glinted behind their lenses. Damn those glasses! He could be wearing a mask for all she could read his expression.

'Congratulations,' the registrar said, and Sandra resisted the urge to say none were called for as she turned to the impassive man who was now her husband.

The wedding reception remained a blur to her—the result of two glasses of champagne gulped down too fast—and the next thing she knew she was hugging her father goodbye and saying farewell to the few relatives and friends gathered to attend this rushed wedding. They probably figured she was pregnant and wanted to be a wife before she became a mother! Knowing Randall as she did, Sandra found the idea laughable. He was too in command of himself to allow such an accident to happen!

It wasn't until they arrived at Heathrow and were met by a barrage of photographers that she appreciated that in marrying Randall Pearson—who ran her father's empire—she had become newsworthy.

'When did you realise you were in love...?' 'Will you give your husband your voting shares...?' 'When...?' 'Why...?' 'How...?' 'What...?'

The questions came fast and furious and Sandra was at a loss for words, anxious not to give the wrong answers, and relieved when Randall fielded them for her with good humour, then unceremoniously pushed a way for them through the Departure Hall to the private lounge that served Concorde passengers.

'We'll probably have a repeat performance the other side,' he warned. 'And they'll be even tougher to shake off there.'

'You did a good job here,' she said, then added waspishly, 'I dare say you enjoyed every minute of it.'

'Enjoyed it?'

'Letting the world know what a brilliant marriage you've made!'

'*You* didn't do too badly either!'

His sarcastic retort startled her, and aware of it, his mouth curled sardonically.

'Two can play the same game, Sandra, so be warned.'

She lapsed into silence, maintaining it for most of the four-hour flight across the Atlantic.

As Randall had predicted, they were met by an equally vociferous media contingent at Kennedy Airport. Only this time they were protected by burly security men who elbowed a path for them to a waiting limousine.

Only when settled in its quiet confines and purring along the freeway did Sandra realise she was trembling, and that her hands were clenched into tight fists.

'Relax,' Randall said quietly. 'The ordeal's over.'

'For me it's only begun!'

'You have an innate ability to be cutting,' he said conversationally. 'Lucky for you I don't bleed easily!'

'You can't force me to be nice to you.'

'As you've already made clear. So please don't repeat yourself. You married me to please your father, and I married you to please myself!'

'You'll *have* to please yourself,' she rejoined tartly. 'I won't do it for you.'

Surprisingly he laughed. 'A rather risqué suggestion, dear wife, and one I won't obey!'

She coloured to the roots of her hair, and resolutely stared through the window for the rest of the journey.

It was early afternoon, New York time, when they reached the Pierre Hotel, overlooking Central Park. It was among the most prestigious in Manhattan, and their suite the most luxurious—consisting of two bedrooms and bathrooms, and a sitting-room furnished in Louis Quinze style.

But neither the size nor the décor impressed Sandra as much as the huge bowls of freesias whose delicate colour and fragrance delighted the eye and nose. Were they from the management?—Randall stayed here regularly, she knew.

'I hope you don't think it's overdone?' His voice cut across her thoughts.

'No—they're wonderful. Who sent them?'

'Most brides would have guessed.'

'I'm not like most brides,' she said quickly, 'so I didn't anticipate your behaving like a bridegroom.'

'More's the pity. I realise you don't regard us as a loving couple, but I haven't given you cause to hate me.'

'I don't. It's myself I hate for letting you manipulate me.'

'Manipulate you?' He came so close to her that she saw the silver flecks in his eyes, bright-hard as diamond chips, and a sure sign of anger—totally unlike the smoky grey they had been earlier that morning when he had placed the wedding ring on her finger.

'May I remind you,' he went on, 'that *you* are the one who told your father we were engaged?'

'I must have been out of my mind!'

His reply was forestalled by the ringing of the telephone, and after a brief conversation he informed her that his New York assistant was waiting for him downstairs.

'I'll go to my bedroom, then,' Sandra said, anticipating that Randall would invite him to the suite.

'There's no need. I'll see him in the bar. You might as well have a rest while I'm gone, or you'll be tired by this evening.'

Taking his advice, she nodded and went to her room, where she relaxed on the bed, convinced she wouldn't sleep and startled when, what seemed to be a moment later,

an overhead light beamed down on her.

Shocked, she sat up, seeing Randall at the door.

'I knocked, but you were dead to the world,' he apologised, 'and snoring pretty as a piglet!'

'I don't snore!' she said indignantly.

'You've a funny singing voice, then!'

Against her will she chuckled. 'What time is it?'

'British or American?'

'American,' she said. 'The quicker you get used to it, the better.'

'It's seven, and I suggest you get ready for dinner. They eat early this side of the Atlantic.'

'We're dining together?' she said, surprised. 'I thought you'd be tied up?'

'Tied up?' he enquired.

'Oh, come on, Randall! This is a business trip, not a honeymoon.'

'It's both, and I intend making it look as if it is.' He came further into the room. 'I won't have our marriage be fodder for the gossips.'

'Frightened they'll rake up something from your past?'

'I've nothing to be ashamed of, though I'd hardly say the same of *yours*.'

Warily Sandra eyed him. 'What's *that* supposed to mean?'

'Barry,' came the succinct reply.

'Spying on me, Randall?' Relief flooded her, though she was careful to hide it. 'Is that how you get your kicks?'

'It had nothing to do with me. Your father had you watched—for your own safety I might add. We live in dangerous times, Sandra, and you're worth your weight in diamonds.'

She reined in her temper, knowing he spoke the truth, and abhorring the shackles it put on her life.

'What else do you know about me?' she demanded. 'The name of my hairdresser, where I buy my clothes? The legion of men I've slept with?'

His lips curled with amusement. 'You might be less unsure of yourself if you had! No, I put it at two or three, and not greatly proficient either. Had they been, you wouldn't be such a mass of self-doubt.'

He raised his hand and lightly stroked a strand of her silky blonde hair. 'So beautiful and so untouched,' he said softly. 'What a waste!'

He left the room as swiftly as he had entered, and Sandra lay motionless for a moment, wondering what he would say if he knew she hadn't had *any* lovers, let alone two or three! He was remarkably perceptive where she was concerned, and it worried her. She hadn't expected him to be and it made her conscious of him in a way she did not like. Was it because he was now her husband and, according to their marriage vows, should be joined to her in body as well as mind?

Her fingers went to her hair, stroking it as he had done. He had promised to make no demands on her, yet this last scene with him rang a warning bell in her brain. One wrong word or look from her could provoke him to anger, and since men often resorted to the physical when their tempers were aroused, it would behove her to take no chances. Yet surely Randall was too calculating to let any woman move him to unrestrained passion?

The thought wasn't as reassuring as it might have been, for it suddenly struck her he might well decide that bedding her was his best way of keeping her. If he tried, would she be able to restrain him? He was adept at kissing—that much she knew—so it was on the cards he would be equally adept as a lover. Not that sexual prowess meant warmth. It was merely a hunger to be appeased, and there was no reason to doubt that in this respect his appetite was no different from that of most other men.

Curiosity stirred in her about his private life and the women he had known since the night—all those years ago—she had turned him down. She had never heard any gossip about him, which either meant he was not worth gossiping about, or was extremely discreet. She'd take a bet it was the latter, for he was a man who gave away nothing of himself.

Pity she wasn't the same. In that sense Randall could teach her a thing or two, and she would be wise to learn from him.

With little enthusiasm, Sandra showered and changed into an amber silk dress, darker than her hair, lighter than her eyes which glowed like jewels in long-lashed fringes. Determined not to look the child he had called her, she piled her hair on top of her head, pleased at how sophisticated it made her appear, though the style accentuated her loss of weight, and she dabbed extra colour on to her high cheekbones to draw attention from the hollows beneath them.

Randall was waiting for her in the sitting-room, austere in a dark suit—naturally!—of some silky material that emphasised his height. He was nursing a drink, but did not offer her one. Instead he set down his glass and, crossing to the small cupboard in the lobby, took out a darkly glowing sable coat.

'My wedding gift to you.' He placed it around her shoulders. 'I'm sorry I couldn't give it to you this morning, but I had it made here. The styling's so much better.'

Was it indeed? And how many furs had he bought for other women that he could be so expert?

'I don't wear animal skins,' she said, taking it off and enjoying his startled look. But not for long, for he came back at her fast.

'You wear leather shoes and eat meat, don't you? So what's the difference?'

She was still floundering for an answer when he draped the coat over her shoulders again and opened the door for her.

In silence they went down to the chauffeur-driven limousine waiting for them.

'It's a nuisance bothering with taxis,' Randall explained, helping her in. 'They're always there when the sun's shining, but come rain or rush hour, they're like virgins in a brothel—non-existent!'

It was hard for her not to smile and, glimpsing the dimple that came and went in her cheek, he half sighed.

'Do you find it so difficult to relax with me, Sandra? We'll hardly be a picture of newly wedded bliss if we're constantly at each other's throats.'

'I couldn't care less what picture we make.'

'Your father will.'

Damn Randall for hitting at her Achilles' heel. And he knew he had too, as his smile confirmed.

'Putting on an act doesn't come easily to me, Randall.'

'In one way I'm glad to hear it.'

She tried to ignore the nuance in his tone, but could not prevent a flush rising in her cheeks. Again he was quick to see it, as the widening of his smile showed.

'We sometimes have to do things contrary to our nature,' he went on. 'But surely being friends with me isn't such an outlandish thought?'

It wasn't. In these past weeks Sandra had come to appreciate his agile mind, the perceptive comments he made in his deceptively quiet way. Whoever had said 'still waters run deep' must definitely have had Randall in mind!

His suggestion that they be friends, though a sensible one, held danger for her, for if she weakened on this, she might weaken on other things. Yet it would be wearing to live with him in a perpetual state of tension, to say nothing of the possibility that her father might hear of it.

'Very well,' she said. 'I'll try to play it your way.'

The car stopped in front of a golden brown canopy, where a commissionaire, beating his arms against the cold wind blowing down Eighty-First Street, hurried forward to open the door.

The restaurant was exactly what she had expected Randall to choose: elegant, discreet, with excellent French food.

Although she had agreed to call a truce, she had no intention of overdoing it. But two glasses of 1957 Chambertin and she was filled with such blissful lethargy it was impossible to maintain her aloofness.

'This restaurant reminds me of you,' she declared. 'It's special in an understated way.'

Randall's eyes gleamed behind his glasses. 'So I'm special, eh?'

'Special as in unique—thank heavens there's only one of you!'

He burst out laughing, head thrown back, and she was surprised to see how strong his neck was.

'I should have known you didn't mean it as a compliment!' he added when he could speak, 'but I'll take it as one.'

'Why?'

'Ask me that question in a year and I'll tell you.'

'Tell me now,' she pressed, and was only aware of leaning forward when she saw his eyes lower to the full curve of her breasts. Hastily she straightened and averted her eyes. 'I don't really want to know. I was just making conversation.'

'That's something you need never bother doing.'

Was he making another crack at her?

'No, I'm not,' he said, divining her thoughts. 'I was stating a fact. I've never regarded silence as something that has to be broken. Talking too much is one of the banes of modern life.'

Her thoughts went instantly to Barry, who was a nonstop talker. If she had wanted to choose two more dissimilar men, she couldn't have found them if she'd tried!

But it was lucky she had, for Randall could never remind her of the man she loved. Not that she needed reminding. Resolutely she concentrated on her meal, and they finished it in silence.

In silence too they returned to the hotel, and crossing the lobby she saw a young couple entering the elevator ahead of them, young and clearly in love, if their clasped hands and intent looks were anything to go by. Self-pity welled up in her, and she quickened her step, so anxious to be alone in her room that she half tripped. Randall's hand shot out to steady her, his fingers sliding up the wide fur sleeve. Instantly she pulled free, and though he must have noticed it, he made no comment.

The intimacy of their lamplit sitting-room brought home to her how happy she could have been had she been wearing Barry's ring. Yet as the thought came, she railed at her stupidity. The Barry she had believed she knew didn't exist. The real man was a womaniser incapable of deep feeling. That was one good thing about her marriage to Randall: it had saved her from an even worse one!

'Don't look so downcast,' he chided. 'Things always look worse at three o'clock in the morning.'

'It isn't three——' Sandra stopped. 'How silly of me! I was forgetting the time change.'

'A good night's sleep and things will look far less gloomy.'

'They're bright and glowing for *you*,' she couldn't help saying. 'You must be delighted with yourself.'

'Do I look delighted?'

She took in the silvery fair hair, the pale skin and firmly compressed mouth. 'You look as you always do, Randall—closed and shuttered behind your glasses— which is how I want you to stay!'

Stalking into her room, she closed the door and made an obvious noise locking it. Let him know she didn't trust him; let him know that though he was her husband, she would never be his wife in anything other than name.

CHAPTER SEVEN

SANDRA spoke to her father daily, and he sounded so much brighter that she called Dr Baxter to make certain he wasn't putting on an act.

'Absolutely not,' the doctor confirmed. 'He's making excellent progress and I've never seen him happier.'

Because of me, Sandra knew, and her spirits lifted. With it came a surge of energy that sent her out of the hotel into the elegant atmosphere of uptown Fifth Avenue, with its fur-coated women and lapdogs. Poodles were in fashion this year, apricot, blue-grey, and brown fur matching the sables and minks that lined the shower-proof raincoats. Only the nouveau-riches wore their furs on the outside these days!

Belting her vicuna coat tighter around her, she set off for the Guggenheim. It was crazy to mope her life away; she might as well make the most of her stay in New York, a city she had, until now, viewed mainly through stores, restaurants and taxis.

'I envy you,' Randall said one morning as she came into the sitting-room with a guide book. 'I've lost count of the times I've been here, yet all I ever get to see is Wall Street and boardrooms!'

'Why exactly are we here now? You've never told me.'

'I didn't think you were interested.' He glanced at his wrist watch. 'Unfortunately I can't spare the time to answer you, but I'll be happy to do so later.'

Hoping he wouldn't remember, for she was convinced he'd go into a boring, long-winded business explanation, she slipped on her coat.

'Where are you off to this morning?' he enquired as they went down to the lobby together and out into the crisp air.

'The Staten Island Ferry, if it isn't too cold. Otherwise I'll explore Greenwich Village.'

'Make sure you keep to the safe parts,' he warned. 'The crime rate here is worse than in London.'

'Stop treating me like a child!'

'Stop behaving like one.'

Sandra set her lips tight and counted to ten, and almost as if he knew what she was doing, he grinned. It took years off his age and she blurted out, 'You should smile more often. You look far nicer.'

'A compliment this early in the morning?'

'It's safer than late at night,' she said with rare teasing.

'Don't you believe it. I'm a night *and* morning man!'

Scarlet-faced, she hailed a cab.

'Take the car,' said Randall behind her.

With a shake of her head she climbed into the dingy interior, breathing a sigh of relief as it sped away from the kerb. Whatever had got into her, making such a suggestive remark to him? But his reply had been even more suggestive, and it lingered in her mind, sending little tremors through her, and reminding her that she was twenty-two and untouched, yet hungry for love.

Except that with Randall it would be lust. She was wryly amused that such an old-fashioned word had come into her head; but then Randall was an old-fashioned man in many ways, so different from—damn! She absolutely wasn't going to think of Barry. Nor Randall either, for that matter. New York lay before her, and she intended devoting herself to exploring its delights.

She was a fearless sightseer, going further afield as her curiosity widened, to include The Cloisters, Rhode Island, and the tranquillity of sea-breezed enclaves on the far reaches of Long Island. But inevitably she enjoyed returning to New York, with its incredible skyline, swanky department stores, museums and art galleries.

She enjoyed shopping too. Having camouflaged her true identity over the past few years, she indulged herself now, and soon the walk-in closet in her hotel suite was crammed with designer clothes. Not that she had much occasion to wear them, for Randall only managed the occasional dinner with her, generally leaving her to dine alone.

The first few times she ate in the suite then, tiring of looking at the same four walls, she had gone to the dining-room. But even in this exclusive hotel several men had tried to pick her up, and she had found it less hassle to remain upstairs.

This went on for ten days, and on the evening of the eleventh she decided enough was enough; pick-up or not, she would take herself to a restaurant. She knew all the important ones, having been to them with her father, but not fancying opulent surroundings, was debating whether to ask reception downstairs if they could recommend a smaller, good one, when Randall sauntered in, unbuttoning his shirt and loosening his tie as he made for the whisky decanter. His pallor bespoke long hours of discussion in rooms where fresh air—as opposed to air-conditioned—was as rare as butterflies in Central Park.

'Doing anything special tonight?' he asked.

What a stupid question. 'Yes. I'm dining at the British Embassy in Washington, then attending a concert at the Kennedy Centre!'

'Sorry,' he said wryly, 'I deserved the sarcasm. Guess I'm not thinking straight. But after five solid hours talking...'

He drained his glass, then sank into an armchair. His body was flacid, his hands limp at his sides. His undone collar revealed a faintly paler line of skin, and as he undid another button of his shirt, the better to rub his neck, Sandra glimpsed a faint fuzz of soft brown hair.

Quickly she looked away, disturbed by his rare vulnerability. Randall, vulnerable? There were many words she could apply to him, but that wasn't one of them!

'Hungry?' he asked.

'Not particularly. Why?'

'If you don't mind waiting an hour, I'll have a catnap and a shower and take you to dinner.'

'There's no need.'

'I thought we were going to try to be friends,' he said softly, and she realised he had misinterpreted her answer.

'I wasn't being rude, Randall. It's just that you look more in need of a good sleep than taking me out.'

'I need something to relax me,' he said, rising and stretching. 'I might even do without a catnap.'

'No,' she said impulsively. 'I'm not in a hurry. If we don't eat till nine, it's fine with me.'

'I'll be ready by eight,' he promised, and was as good as his word, returning to the living-room on the dot, skin flushed from his shower, hair still damp and looking a
little darker because of it.

'You must have been extremely fair-haired as a child,' she said.

'Ash-blond. Acceptable in a girl, but at a tough boarding school I came in for a hell of a lot of teasing.'

It was hard to imagine him a child, and she wondered if he had been as contained then as he was now.

'I was always fighting because of it,' he added, negating her train of thought, 'and ended up in the school boxing team.'

'No cauliflower ears or broken nose, I see!'

'The other boys had that!'

She laughed, and there was still an air of ease between them as they took their table in a candlelit restaurant whose windows afforded a panoramic view of the

Hudson River. It was a place for lovers: soft lights and softer music, tables set discreetly apart, food and service faultless.

Fearing he was out to charm her—if such a term could be applied to him—Sandra resolutely held herself aloof, and was disconcerted when it seemed nothing was further from his mind, for his conversation centred on his take-over of an American drug company.

It was the first time Randall had discussed business with her, for though he had promised to do so a few days ago, he had not followed it through. That he was doing it now showed what a delicate stage the talks were at—which was probably why he was using her as a sounding board. Aware of this, she pretended interest, but gradually his drily witty account captured her attention. He made the take-over seem as suspense-full as a thriller, and by all accounts there were several villains in it intent on thwarting him.

'No fight for a company is ever bloodless,' he agreed, when she said as much. 'Heads inevitably roll.'

'Never yours. I'm sure it's too firmly fixed.'

'Glad you think so. But no one's invincible.'

'You're not saying Harris Pharmaceuticals could be taken over, are you?' she asked.

'Everything's possible.' Randall signed the bill and they rose to leave. 'The larger and more successful a company, the greater the danger of being swallowed up by an even bigger one!'

'You're too clever to let that happen.'

'I hope so,' he said matter-of-factly, escorting her to their limousine.

'Even if we were bought out, I'm sure you'd still be left to run the company,' she said. 'My father thinks you're terrific.'

'His daughter doesn't!'

'We aren't talking personally.'

'Agreed.' He paused, then added, 'I'd never stay in this job if I didn't have full control. And not because I like being top dog as you obviously think, but because I follow a policy which most of the big drug companies don't.'

'Which is?'

'To sell certain essential drugs at rock-bottom prices.'

'Really?' She was amazed. 'How do we manage to keep our profits so high?'

'Because our salaries are modest by comparison with our rivals, and we run a tight ship. No over-staffing, no big expense accounts and a wonderfully loyal research team.'

'I'd no idea. Daddy always kept me in the dark about these things.'

'He probably didn't think you'd be interested.'

'Until tonight I wasn't,' she admitted as they reached the Pierre and went up to their suite. 'But you make it sound so alive and exciting, I'd like to learn more.'

'From now on I'll keep you in the picture,' he promised. 'It's a pity you never came into the company. You're bright enough to have proved yourself within six months.'

'It wouldn't have worked, Randall. The stories of daughters stepping into their fathers' shoes remain stories—and on the best-seller lists! But in real life it rarely happens.'

'Hefner's daughter ran *Playboy*, and there's a very feminine head of Cartiers,' Randall stated.

'There are always exceptions,' Sandra agreed, 'but I never saw myself as exceptional.'

'I wish you wouldn't run yourself down.'

Reluctant to explain that her complex had started because she hadn't been the son her father had wanted, she changed the subject. 'If this take-over goes through, will you have to spend more time here?'

'Yes, indeed. We'll be here about three or four months a year.'

'We?'

'I'm not leaving you behind. In the words of the song, "I've grown accustomed to your face".'

'After only three weeks?'

'You've been in my mind longer than that.'

Abruptly she moved to her room. 'I'm going to bed. I've an early hair appointment.'

'Don't ever have it cut short. I——' He stopped. 'Stupid of me. I should know that's a sure way of making you chop it off!'

'I would,' she laughed, 'except that *I* like it long too! I'm also replenishing my wardrobe,' she added, 'so if you've any preference as to colour and style, I'll be happy to ignore them!'

'I like everything you wear. You've excellent taste.'

'Huh! I bet you haven't noticed a thing I've worn here.'

'Try me.'

'OK. What was I wearing last night?'

'Green chiffon, with shoes to match.'

'Very good. And the night before?'

'An amber dress in some clingy material, and a few nights earlier, something similar, only in red. Then there was the blue, slit to the waist down the back—very enticing, I might add—then a black with a deep cleavage—even more enticing. Also two suits, one a cinnamon mixture, and the other——'

'Enough!' she cried. 'I can see you've a photographic memory.'

'Only for things I want to remember.' He rose to accompany her to the door. 'Want me to wake you in the morning?'

'No, thanks. The operator will.'

He was gone when Sandra went into the sitting-room for breakfast, and was still absent when she returned later that afternoon laden with packages. What an ex-

travagant day it had been! Exhilarating too, and she
didn't regret a minute of it, nor a penny spent. A penny?
That was a joke! She couldn't remember ever spending
so much.

Wandering to the dressing-table she picked up her
hairbrush, appreciating the pleasure of being young and
carefree, of having her whole life ahead of her! She
stopped, brush mid-air as a shaft of sunlight caught her
wedding ring. Well, not quite carefree. There was still
Randall, though admittedly their marriage was turning
out far better than she had anticipated.

But she couldn't see it continuing on this even tenor.
Sooner or later he'd make a move to consummate it, and
then what would she do? Fight or flight, or give in?
Today she wasn't as sure which choice she'd make as
she had been a month ago. Involuntarily she visualised
herself in his arms, his hands caressing her, his lips
moving down her body... Colour flooded her face, and
with a shaking hand she continued brushing her hair.

'No need to ask if you've had a successful day,'
Randall said behind her, and through the mirror she saw
him looking amusedly at the boxes and packages on the
bed and chairs.

'Yours seems to have been successful too,' Sandra
commented, watching his unsteady gait.

'The deal's signed and we had a little celebration,' he
explained.

'Not so little,' she said, aware of his alcohol-scented
breath.

'Too true. A vintage brandy that was highly tempting.'
His voice was slightly slurred. 'It's given me one hell of
a headache!'

'Shall I ring for some tea, or would you prefer something else?'

'Only you,' he said huskily, and reached out for her.

She knew better than to resist, especially in his present
state, and she remained passive, hoping he would get the

message. But he didn't, and drew her closer, pressing his mouth firmly down on hers. It was warm and soft, though as the kiss lengthened, the warmth became heat, and the softness a pulsating pressure she found difficult to resist. Yet resist it she must, and she forced her eyes open, hoping the sight of Randall's face, so near, would help retain her strength of mind.

But it had the opposite effect, for it made her aware of the silky texture of his hair, soft as a baby's, and the translucence of his eyelids. She couldn't remember him taking off his glasses. His skin had a faint tinge of pinkness too, seen so close, and her nostrils savoured the scent of the man himself, a scent that had nothing to do with aftershave or alcohol, but was the very essence of him.

Involuntarily her hands touched the side of his face, and Randall trembled and caught them in a tight grasp, then drew them down to his chest. Even through his shirt she felt the heat of his body, and her own responded to it with an overwhelming wave of desire that drew her to him like a magnet, that made her seek the touch of his lips, open her mouth to the demand of his tongue, and let him lead her unresistingly to the bed.

Aflame with desire, Sandra moaned in delight as he slipped her dress from her and ran his hands across her satin-smooth skin. The cool man had gone, replaced by one consumed by a passion he made no attempt to hide as he pressed her back hard against the coverlet and devoured her with his eyes. Colour bloomed in her cheeks and she lowered her lids. Her shyness inflamed him the more, and he muttered incoherently in his throat as his lips fastened around one rose-tipped nipple and he suckled it with his tongue, while all the while his fingers sought the hidden crevices of her body, moving lightly and tenderly until they homed in on to the downy mound between her thighs, then probed deep to find the hidden bud that pulsed alive at his touch.

She gasped at the sudden ecstasy it aroused in her, and grasped her legs tightly together. For an instant his hand was still, then as her muscles relaxed, his finger moved again, gently probing and rubbing, sending such delicious tremors coursing through her that she abandoned herself to the sensual waves washing over her.

Her tongue rubbed against his, its movement mimicking the movement of his fingers and, aware of it, he slid his other hand down her back to her buttocks, grasping the rounded curves and pressing her close upon him. His weight was heavy, but she did not care, and as she felt the sinewy length of him, her legs parted and lifted to twine themselves around his. With a deep sigh he lay between them, then half turned his head so that it rested on the pillow next to hers, their mouths still fused together.

Caught in her own desire, victim of her own need, she let her hands flutter down his back, enchanted by the hard smoothness and the strength of the muscled thighs. Yet even as she became aware of them, they softened beneath her touch, and at the same time his mouth eased its pressure and relaxed away from hers. Surprised, she drew back a fraction and opened her eyes, astonishment overcoming her as she saw he had fallen fast asleep.

So much for her allure!

Chagrin fought with amusement and amusement won, though this was almost instantly replaced by fury. Not with Randall but with herself for responding to him. How could she have played into his hands like that? Visualising how triumphant he would have been had he actually managed to claim her, Sandra thanked fate for preventing it. Though perhaps she should have thanked the vintage brandy he had consumed at the celebratory signing of the merger!

Carefully she eased herself from the bed and went into the bathroom. Glimpsing her reflection, she despised herself for the hectic flush on her cheeks, and her mouth still swollen by Randall's kisses. Furiously she rubbed it with the back of her hand. How could she have been so abandoned with him? She must have been mad!

Or was it madness to be physically attracted to a good-looking, intelligent man who also happened to be her husband? And was it because he *was* her husband that she hadn't felt the overwhelming fear of sex which an aroused man had always engendered in her? Amazement at having forgotten the trauma that Mario had caused in her life made her relive her passionate response to Randall, and as she did, she writhed with shame at her behaviour.

Jumping up, she stepped into the shower and let the cool water spray hard on her body, as if hoping to wash away Randall's touch. But no amount of water could erode memory and, outwardly cool but inwardly seething, she dried herself, put on her négligé and tiptoed back into the bedroom. Randall was still asleep and she moved closer to the bed and surveyed him. She could not remember him undressing—any more than she could remember him undressing her, and with the eyes of an artist, she allowed her gaze to roam his body. It was as perfectly formed as she had known it would be: wide-shouldered, narrow-hipped with long, lean flanks. Hard to believe his job was a sedentary one. Even as she watched him, he stirred, and she drew back swiftly, though he did not awaken, merely shifted on to his back and flung out an arm.

His features were softened by repose, but they were still firm, though the faint lines she had frequently seen on his brow had disappeared, and he looked unusually young. She frowned. He was only five years older than Barry, yet somehow he seemed far more.

Barry! Where had *he* been this past half-hour? Not in her mind, that was for sure! Mortified by this further evidence of how easily she had succumbed to physical desire, Sandra quickly ran from the room, but she could

not run from her thoughts nor the questions clamouring
to be answered. Why had she allowed Randall an intimacy she had refused Barry? Was it really because of
the meaningless ring on her finger? Yet maybe the ring
wasn't meaningless after all, for it at least signified a
legal joining together of a man and a woman, which
Barry, for all his assurances of love, had resisted.

Whatever the reason for her present behaviour, she
was glad that the natural outcome had been forestalled,
for
had she succumbed to Randall in passion, she would
have hated herself when reason returned. For reason told
her that Randall would have seen his possession of her
as a victory, another take-over successfully completed!

For an instant she was filled with despair, not knowing
how long this empty marriage had to continue, or if she
could go on holding him at arm's length. He had made
it clear he would not let the platonic state continue in-
definitely, and she now knew that if he forced himself
upon her, she would find it hard not to respond to him.

What a galling thought! She almost screamed with the
frustration of it, but instead thumped a cushion with all
her might. The physical exertion left her panting but
surprisingly more sanguine—certainly with sufficient
composure to call down to the switchboard and ask them
to hold all calls for the next two hours. Then she settled
herself on the sofa and made her mind a blank. Thoughts
of Randall persisted, but she pushed them resolutely
aside, intent only on remaining calm and logical. No
one could control her unless she allowed it, and though
she was Randall's wife, she was determined to remain
her own mistress!

On this thought she fell asleep.

CHAPTER EIGHT

RANDALL was still dead to the world when Sandra went into her room two hours later. He was lying on his side again, and the line and indent of his back and leg made her long to sketch him. Disturbed by the thought, she hurriedly collected her clothes for the evening and went into the bathroom to dress.

She was putting on lipstick and debating whether to wake him when the telephone did it for her. She heard Randall answer it—his voice still heavy with sleep—and waited till the receiver was replaced before returning to the bedroom. He had pulled the coverlet over him and was sitting up, hair in place, glasses on.

Back in business, she thought wryly, but said nothing.

'That was Glenning—chairman of the company I've just bought,' he explained. 'He's been trying to get me for an hour.'

'Blame me for that. You were sleeping so soundly, I asked reception to hold calls.'

'Not entirely unexpected from a honeymoon suite,' he murmured. 'Though if memory serves me right, I was a somewhat exhausted bridegroom!'

'Luckily,' she added.

'You'd have stopped me?'

'Eventually.' With a supreme effort she managed to sound coolly amused. 'I was being a tease, I'm afraid—curious to see how far you'd go.'

'All the way, if it hadn't been for that damned brandy,' he said bluntly.

'I'd have kneed you first!' she said equally bluntly. 'When I give myself to a man, it will be willingly or not at all. Remember that, Randall.'

'And you remember I'm your husband, and intend being a real one sooner rather than later.'

Without embarrassment he flung aside the coverlet and stood up. She drew back sharply and his smile was tight.

'Don't be scared, Sandra. When I decide to make you mine, it won't be through rape.'

'That's the only way you'll get me!'

'I think not.'

Remembering her earlier ardent response to him, she hastily looked away. 'Do you have another meeting tonight?'

'Unfortunately, yes. I've several points to discuss with Glenning, but I'll try to get away by nine. If you like we can go to a disco.'

'A disco?' she echoed.

'I'm full of surprises! Wait till you know me better!' He walked out before she could reply.

When she entered the sitting-room a while later he was already there, in a charcoal-grey suit, cream shirt and maroon tie. He appeared completely revitalised and Sandra's pulses quivered in a way she didn't like. What a relief it would be when they returned to England and a normal life. Living in such proximity to him—at least in his home there'd be staff around—was getting to her. She stiffened as he came nearer, the spicy scent of his aftershave drawing her eyes to his newly shaved chin.

'Twice a day,' she blurted out.

'What?'

She went scarlet, but shouldered on. 'You've shaved again.'

'I don't usually,' he agreed, the tilt of his mouth making his reason obvious.

'Don't push your luck,' she snapped.

'You can't blame me for being an optimist!'

'It'll do you more good to be a realist.'

He laughed. 'I enjoy provoking you, Sandra. You've an amusing line in retorts.'

With a toss of her head she stalked ahead of him out of their suite.

'If I'm delayed,' he said as they reached the lobby, 'I'll call you.'

'Don't you ever get fed up with business?'

'There are times when I could do without it,' he said drily. 'Our honeymoon being one.'

'It's not a honeymoon.'

'It almost was.' Randall ignored her blush. 'If I could have spent more time with you, we'd have got to know each other better. It isn't easy learning to live with a person and accepting their habits and foibles.'

'I can't imagine you with foibles,' she replied. 'To me, you're the original faceless man.' His lips tightened and she added quickly, 'That's ruder than I meant it to be. It's just that you're always so controlled and——'

'No need to explain,' he cut across her.

She could see he was still put out and found it vaguely disturbing. Yet why should she care? If he wanted emotional happiness he should have married someone else!

They were nearing the dining-room when Sandra heard a lilting voice call his name, and saw a petite redhead in black chiffon coming towards them. In her early thirties, she had a serene, Madonna-like face, and except for a faint weariness around the eyes was a remarkably lovely woman, her smile devoid of artifice, her charm palpable enough to be felt the instant of meeting her.

'Randall!' She extended long slim hands to him. 'How marvelous to see you. I'd no idea you were in New York.'

'I'm on business and my honeymoon.'

There was an instant of startled silence before the woman spoke. 'You're married! That's incredible. Why didn't you let me know?'

'I tried, but you'd left for Australia.' His hand was firm on Sandra's arm. 'Sandra, this is Aileen, widow of Dominic Royston, who was my closest friend.'

Sandra barely managed to hide her surprise that Randall had known the artist whose death in a yachting accident two years before had been such a great loss to the art world.

'I still can't believe you're married,' the woman said to Randall, her sherry-brown eyes appraising Sandra warmly. 'I'm delighted someone's finally managed to hook him. He's far too nice a fish to be left swimming in the sea.'

Sandra let a slight smile speak for her. She could hardly say she would have preferred the fish to swim in the sea for ever!

'How come you're here?' Randall intervened, giving Aileen an affectionate hug. Sandra was amazed. She knew he was capable of passion, but not such spontaneous warmth!

'I flew in for the opening of Dominic's exhibition,' Aileen answered him. 'You can't imagine the prices his paintings are fetching!'

'I can. And it's no more than he deserved.'

The soft mouth trembled momentarily, then firmed as the woman drew away from Randall. 'How remiss of me to keep you. I look forward to seeing you both in England.'

'Why not in New York?' Randall grinned.

'You're on——'

'A honeymoon-cum-business trip,' he repeated. 'Which means Sandra's often left to her own devices.'

'Maybe we can have dinner one evening?' Aileen suggested, turning to Sandra.

'What's wrong with now?' asked Randall. 'I'm on my way to a meeting. I'm sure Sandra would enjoy some company.'

'Mrs Royston might be tied up,' said Sandra quickly, feeling a bit like a parcel nobody wanted.

'On the contrary,' the woman smiled. 'I'd decided I'd had my fill of agents and buyers and deserved an evening without them. I'd love to have dinner with you.'

Randall moved ahead of them to arrange a table for two, and Sandra, turning to Aileen, saw her watching him with such an expression of longing that she averted her eyes. Were she and Randall only friends, or had there been more between them? It was an intriguing question, and one her dinner with Aileen tonight might answer.

'All fixed.' Randall returned to them. 'I'll be back as soon as I can.'

The flurry of taking their seats and ordering drinks overcame Sandra's initial discomfort at being with an almost complete stranger, and in next to no time they were chatting amicably.

'Have you known Randall long?' she asked the woman.

'We met at my engagement party. Well, hardly a party,' Aileen chuckled. 'There were only the three of us. Dominic wasn't famous then, and we were living in an attic in Fulham. We climbed out on to the roof and celebrated with sausages, chips and champagne! Randall brought the champagne, I might add!' The grin widened. 'Even those days he was climbing high.'

'Where did *they* meet?' Sandra asked.

'At university. Dominic dropped out after the first year and went to art school, but they stayed friends. Randall used to get very irritated because Dom wouldn't accept help from him—he wanted to make it on his own.'

'He certainly succeeded!'

'He did, didn't he? I'm glad he lived to see some success.' Sherry brown eyes misted over. 'But enough about me. Tell me about you and Randall. I saw him two months ago and the beast never said a word about you!'

'It was all rather sudden, though we've known each other for years. Randall works for my father's company,' Sandra explained.

'Good lord!' Aileen's expression said much more, and Sandra concentrated on the menu, their conversation only resuming when they had given their orders.

'I hope you'll get Randall to ease up,' the woman went on, spearing a prawn. 'He works too hard.'

'He enjoys it.'

'He always has. He does everything with intensity, doesn't he? Like when he took up flying. He got his pilot's licence sooner than anyone on the course. You've been up in his Cessna, I suppose?'

'I don't like small planes,' Sandra evaded the question. She hadn't even known Randall flew, let alone had his own aircraft!

'He's a superb yachtsman too,' Aileen went on. 'I can't help thinking if he'd been with Dominic that dreadful day...' There was a shake of the red head, and when next she spoke, it was about the success of her husband's exhibition in Sydney.

'I could sell every one of his paintings if I wanted, but I'm taking Randall's advice and holding on to most of them. They've trebled in price in the past two years, and he's positive they'll go even higher.' Another prawn was speared, then set down again. 'But the money's so unimportant to me. I'd give it all away to have Dom back for an hour, to see his face, hold him...' The bright head lifted sharply. 'But how awful of me to be talking so morbidly to you when you're on your honeymoon!'

'Please don't apologise,' Sandra said softly.

But Aileen was in control of herself again and firmly steered the talk away from the past. 'We're neighbours in England, you know. I live ten minutes from Oakland.'

Sandra was about to blurt out that she lived in Wide-acres, miles away, when she remembered she didn't. Her marriage might be a sham, but Randall's home was hers, like it or not.

'Your house is a dream,' Aileen went on. 'But it will be even better with a woman's touch. Randall only used it as a stopover between trips.'

'That will definitely change!' Sandra stated, deliberately speaking as a bride should.

Brown eyes studied her. 'Do you work?'

'I'm a graphic artist.'

'How interesting. Are you——' Aileen broke off as the waiter approached with the sweet trolley. Sandra refused, and Aileen debated between chestnut meringue and *crème brûlée*, finally settling for a small portion of each.

'A sweet tooth?' Sandra smiled.

'Unfortunately.'

'It doesn't show.'

'I wouldn't care if it does,' laughed Aileen.

Sandra knew she meant it, for Aileen was a woman very much at ease with herself. She gave only an impression of beauty, for on closer inspection her features weren't regular enough: nose not quite retroussé, mouth slightly too wide. But her eyes were large and expressive, enhanced by the hint of sadness in their depths.

'Dominic was illustrating a children's book when he died,' she said unexpectedly, 'and his publishers have been at me to have someone else finish it. But I can't bear the thought, so I've shelved the whole thing. I mean, no one could copy his style.' She sighed. 'He was a unique and wonderful man—not only as an artist but as   a   person. I sometimes wish I hadn't loved him so much. At least I wouldn't have found it so hard to get over him.'

Sandra could sympathise, though she herself hadn't ever loved a man with such devotion—not even Barry. Startled by the thought, she frowned. Of course she loved him—yet not with the intensity Aileen had experienced; such oneness of spirit came all too rarely.

'I was lucky to have wonderful friends to help me over my grief,' Aileen confided. 'And Randall in particular. I hope you and I can be friends too. I'm older than you, but——'

'I'm not as young as I look,' Sandra cut in. 'I'm twenty-two.'

'Add ten years for me,' came the reply. 'Though I feel we're on the same wavelength. Anyway, Randall's too intelligent to fall for someone who's just a pretty face.'

You could say that again, Sandra thought with irony, and wondered how Aileen would react if she knew the truth about their marriage. 'You're such a fan of his,' she murmured, 'I'm surprised you and he...' She stopped, appalled at where her tongue had led her.

'Didn't marry?' Aileen finished. 'It wasn't for want of my trying! He's the only person I'd contemplate marrying after Dominic. Unfortunately he only sees me as the widow of his closest friend.'

'If you'd really set your heart on him, I can't see him resisting you.'

'What a lovely thing to say, but you're so wrong. You see, for years he wasn't available.'

Sandra gaped. 'You mean he—he was married before?'

'Heavens, no! He was besotted with some girl who didn't love him. Carried a torch for her for ages!'

Sandra still couldn't believe it. This was an entirely new aspect of Randall's life.

'I always wondered why he remained a bachelor,' she said. 'What happened to the girl?'

'I haven't a clue. Randall was practically a clam where she was concerned. He only mentioned her once to me, years ago, when he was feeling pretty low. But he did let drop that he kept her picture in his desk.'

'Did you ever get to see it?'

'Unfortunately not. But I'm sure she was the reason he became a workaholic.' Aileen flashed her beautiful smile, managing to look apologetic at the same time. 'Randall would have my hide if he knew I'd told you about her. The "other woman" is hardly "bride talk"!'

'I'm not the jealous type,' Sandra said lightly, her mind racing over Randall's cupidity in kidding her father *she* was the love of his life.

'Jealousy doesn't come into it,' she heard Aileen say. 'If Randall had been prepared to settle for second-best he could have had me! No, I only had to see him tonight to know he'd definitely got over her! There's a contentment in his face I haven't seen in years.'

And why shouldn't there be? Sandra thought furiously. He had decided it was profitless wasting his life hankering after someone who didn't want him, and what better than to take a wife who could ensure his security in a company he regarded as his own?

The object of her thoughts suddenly materialised at the entrance to the restaurant. 'Randall's here,' she murmured, watching the tall, self-possessed figure wend its way towards them. 'We'd better drop the subject.'

'I'd be happier if you'd forget it,' whispered Aileen.

'Consider it done,' Sandra assured her, giving Randall a false smile as he reached them. 'Darling! You're back early.'

'I told Glenning I was taking you dancing and it speeded up his thought processes!' He glanced at the table. 'I see you've finished your meal.'

'I was just leaving.' Aileen rose.

'There's no rush. Why don't you join us?'

'A third wheel on a honeymoon?'

'We've had third, fourth and fifth wheels!'

'All the more reason for me to make my departure!'

'How long will you be in New York?' Sandra asked, picking up her purse.

'I'm going to the West Coast tomorrow, and I fly home from there.'

'Then we'll see you in Oakland,' said Randall, standing aside for the two women to walk ahead while he paused at the *maître d*'s desk to settle the bill.

'I've talked too much tonight,' Aileen apologised again to Sandra.

'I'm glad you did. You've given me a much rounder picture of Randall.'

In this respect she wasn't lying, and she was still mulling over what she had learned when she and Randall entered the dimly lit discothèque where exotically dressed couples gyrated to the latest hits.

'You two seemed to hit if off,' Randall commented as they sat down at a corner table.

'I like Aileen. She's much more your kind of woman than I am.'

'I wish you could have known Dominic,' he said, ignoring her comment. 'He was one of the best. A great practical joker too. You'd never believe some of the things we got up to.'

'I can't imagine *you* putting a foot wrong.'

'Several feet, actually!'

'When did you last do anything silly?'

'Never silly,' he corrected. 'Occasionally acted against my better judgement, though.'

'Such as?'

'Marrying you.'

This should have been Sandra's moment of triumph. Randall Pearson had finally done something he regretted! Yet all it gave her was an odd pang of disappointment.

'Let's dance,' he suggested.

Sandra hadn't danced with him since the night of her eighteenth birthday party, and wondered if he had been in love with the other woman then, and had already given up hope of having her. Or had she come on the scene later? Fat chance of satisfying her curiosity, though!

'Hey!'

With a start she saw him waiting for her on the dance floor, and as she went into his arms was tinglingly aware of his nearness. Expecting him to dance with aloof detachment, she was surprised by his excellent sense of rhythm, displaying the pantherlike grace with which he walked. But as the beat quickened, she pulled away from him.

'Mind if we sit this out? It's too fast for me.'

'If I can do it, you can.'

On your own head be it! she thought, and with hair flying and ear-rings swinging, flung herself into the dance. It was frenetic, wild and—surprise, surprise—fun, and she found herself laughing with the sheer joy of it.

Abruptly the tempo slowed, lights dimming to soft pinks and violets as the beat grew languorous. Randall drew her against him, but she held herself rigid, not wanting to succumb to the romantic atmosphere around them as couples snuggled together, cheek touching cheek, hands drifting...

'Relax, my dear. I won't bite!'

He was treating her like a child again, and she said crossly, 'Stop trying to rile me!'

'I didn't mean to. You're my wife and I want you to be happy.'

'The two can never go together!'

'They could if you'd let yourself live in the present instead of the past.'

'I prefer the past. The present is awful, and the future looks worse!'

'Our marriage *could* work,' he persisted, 'but it takes two to tango.'

'Exactly. And you're the last man in the world I want to tango with!'

His answer was to pull her tight against his body, and though she felt the tension in it, outwardly he remained composed. With an effort she concentrated on the music, and gradually her anger lessened and she was able to regard his behaviour with dispassion.

As if he sensed her changed mood, his hand slid down her back, his palm warm through the silk of her dress. Reaching her thigh, he moulded it against his. Sandra half turned her head and her cheek involuntarily brushed his chin.

She bit back a sigh. Although a part of her wanted to dislike him, another found him considerate and kind; certainly kinder to her than her behaviour merited. As he had said, she was as responsible for their marriage as he, and to lay the blame solely on him was unfair.

She glanced at him from the corner of her eye, liking the straight profile, the well-shaped mouth. Was he anxious to make this marriage work in order to offset his failure to get the woman he really wanted? Strange that there was something in life that clever Randall couldn't have.

'I know you think you'll never get over Barry,' he said unexpectedly, 'but take it from me, you will.'

Hell! What right did *he* have to lecture her on un-requited love? 'I'd believe you more easily if I didn't know *you're* still pining for a lost love!' she retorted.

Randall stumbled and muttered beneath his breath. 'Aileen! She's not normally indiscreet.'

'I encouraged her,' Sandra said hastily.

'Looking for my Achilles' heel?'

'Is that surprising? You've no compunction hitting mine.'

'You're right. I'm sorry.'

Taken aback by his apology, she proffered one of her own. 'I agree with what you said earlier, Randall. It's stupid for us to go on fighting. We're stuck with each other for the moment and should make the best of it.'

For answer he drew her close again, but though she relaxed physically, her mind seethed with questions, one of which escaped from her.

'Do you still see her?' she asked.

'Who?'

'The woman you're in love with.'

'Would you care?'

'Why should I?' She could prevaricate too!

'Because you're my wife.'

'Meaningless if it isn't backed by a relationship.'

'Relationship,' he said wryly. 'A woman's favourite word. You make it sound so special, yet one's entire life is spent relating to people and situations—being mature enough to know some things can't be altered to suit one's purpose.'

'And if they can't, to accept second-best,' Sandra concluded. 'As you did with me.'

'I was delighted to accept you.'

'What happens if your lady love suddenly wakes up to what she's missing?'

'You'll be the first to know.'

'But if she——'

'Drop it,' he said curtly. 'It's over.'

Did he mean their conversation or his lost love? But his expression made it plain she'd learn no more from him

and, womanlike, her curiosity grew. Randall no longer fitted into the niche in which she had placed him, for Aileen's disclosure showed him to be fallible, not the calculating machine she had taken him for.

'I'm sorry, Randall. It was mean of me to force you to talk about something you'd rather forget.'

He shrugged. 'I'm pleased you're curious.'

'Pleased?'

'I've finally got an apology out of you!'

'Oh, you——!'

He laughed, and once again pressed the length of his body against hers. The movement of his thighs brought her own to life, reminding her that he was a sensual man to whom her own sensuality responded. It hadn't anything to do with love—it was simply a basic, physical urge.

'How tense you are,' he whispered in her ear. 'I know a sure-fire way of relaxing you!'

'No, thanks.'

'Scared?'

'Only of what it might do to *you*.'

'The thought of it already has!'

In different circumstances his flippancy would have amused her, but the other woman in his life loomed too large, reminding her that she herself was merely a substitute.

'Try a cold shower,' she advised him curtly.

'As a temporary measure only.'

Aware of the warning in his reply, Sandra wondered if she was foolish holding him off. After all, a purely physical relationship could not harm her emotionally— and after her stupidity over Barry, the last thing she wanted was to fall in love. So why not find some pleasure with Randall?

Except for that other woman of his, and his shrewdness in keeping her so well hidden. If he hadn't, he wouldn't have succeeded in marrying the boss's daughter and setting himself up for life!

What a cold-blooded swine he was. Let him settle for that damned photograph in his desk!

CHAPTER NINE

SANDRA almost cheered when Randall told her a few days later that his business was completed and they were free to return home.

'Unless you'd like to stop over for a few days in the Bahamas?' he suggested.

'No, thanks. I'd rather go home.'

'Me too. I've an important meeting Monday morning.'

'You're lucky I didn't take up your offer!'

'If you had, my assistant could have attended the meeting.'

'You mean you aren't indispensable?'

'If I was, you'd soon remind me I wasn't!'

His answer made her ashamed, and she turned away.

They left for London the following morning, Randall studying a batch of documents throughout the flight, and Sandra passing the hours sketching a few of the passengers.

It was late afternoon when they touched down at Heathrow, and as they climbed into the chauffeured car waiting for them, Randall suggested they go direct to Wideacres. 'I'm sure you're anxious to see your father,' he explained.

She nodded and put a grateful hand on his arm. 'You're always very thoughtful.'

'And you're always very surprised by it!'

She smiled. 'That's because your character's like an iceberg most of the time—three-quarters hidden!'

'Icebergs melt, given sufficient warmth.'

She pretended not to hear, and stared through the window as if she had never seen England before!

Certainly she felt none of the joy a bride should feel
coming home from honeymoon. But then why should
she? Where Randall was concerned, her emotions were
like a yo-yo—up and down and then all in a tangle! Only
one thing she knew for certain: no way was she going
to play second fiddle to another woman!

The sight of her father walking slowly across the
drawing-room to greet her sent her problems scattering
like leaves in the wind. *He* was all that mattered to her.
Everyone else could go hang!

She hugged him. 'How much better you look!' though
quite honestly he was a shadow of his former self.

'I never expected you to come here straight from the
airport,' he said gruffly. 'You must be jet-lagged.'

'Concorde's a rest-cure!' Linking her arm through his,
Sandra led him back to his chair.

'Staying to dinner?' he asked after their first flush of
conversation.

'Yes,' Sandra said.

'No,' Randall answered simultaneously, then regarded her quizzically.

'What's it to be?' grinned Edward Harris.

Reminding herself she was supposed to be a loving
wife, she murmured, 'Home, I think.' Then to her father,
'I'll be over to see you tomorrow.'

'Don't be silly. Just knowing you're within driving
distance makes me happy.'

It made her happy too, and she said as much to
Randall when they were finally on their way to Oakland.

'I don't fancy going abroad and leaving him again.
He's so frail.'

'I'm with you there. Though I was hoping we'd spend
a month in Spain before the summer. I've a villa near
Alicante, and there's plenty of room for your father and
a nurse.'

'I didn't realise you had a place abroad.'

'I'll let you have a list of my assets.'

'No need to be sarcastic!'

'I wasn't being. As my wife you're entitled to know.'

Once more she felt ashamed, though a month ago she wouldn't have. Was she going soft in the brain or—or what? Pushing aside the alternative, she said, 'I'm not really your wife, so I don't expect you to tell me anything.'

'Is a permanent future with me still unthinkable?'

'Why put the onus on me?' she demanded. 'Your other love might wake up to what she's missing.'

'I've told you she's in the past. Why can't you forget her? *I* don't give a damn about Barry.'

'Maybe. But I'm not as cold-blooded as you! When a man makes love to me, I don't want to feel I'm a stand-in for someone else.'

'I'd never mistake you for another woman,' came the soft reply. 'Any more than I'd let you mistake me for your erstwhile lover. Once we'd been to bed you'd soon stop thinking of him.'

'How confident you are!'

'Pity *you* aren't.'

She had led with the chin, and pugnaciously he had hit it! She was still smarting when the lights of Oakland came in sight, glowing brightly at the end of a poplar-lined drive.

She had only been here once before—two days after their engagement—and, expecting a formidable mansion, had been delighted by a gem of a small manor house: whitewashed, black-timbered, with solid doors and contentedly puffing chimneystacks. It was a house asking to be filled with love, children and laughter, and it had seemed to her that Randall was cheating it by making her his wife. She felt this even more strongly as she followed him up to the first floor into a charmingly furnished suite consisting of two bedrooms and a bathroom.

'I've a shower off my dressing-room,' he said, 'so you can have the bathroom to yourself.'

'And a suite,' she stated. 'I've no intention of sharing this one with you.'

'And I've no intention of giving the servants food for gossip. You'll be perfectly safe here. All we need share is the entrance foyer.'

Despite his soft tone Sandra knew him well enough to sense his implacability. I must be mad to think he'll give in over anything, she thought. In his own quiet manner he steamrollers over everything.

'You take this room,' he continued, leading her into the main bedroom where silver-grey walls and carpet were a backdrop to sapphire curtains and matching coverlet on the king-size bed. 'If you want to change the colour scheme, feel free.'

'It's fine as it is,' she said indifferently.

'For *you* maybe, not for me!' Unexpectedly savage, Randall strode out and slammed the door.

Well, well, she thought, I'm finally getting to him! It brought a smile to her face and a spring to her step, which remained with her while her luggage was brought in and she helped the Portuguese maid unpack her cases.

She set out silver-framed photographs of her father and her pet dog who had died a year ago—would Randall mind if she bought another? The heck with him, she'd get one anyway! A retriever like Sandy perhaps, or something smaller to sleep on her bed. She giggled— small and snappy in case her husband got ideas!

Looking around, she was amazed at how soon the room took on her personality. But then Randall's was non-existent! Like the silver-grey walls and carpet, it faded into the background. No, that wasn't true. It was always there: quiet, immutable.

She slipped into a black silk trouser suit for dinner— her first meal with her husband in their home, which was so disquieting a thought that it wiped the smile off her face. Not that Randall seemed other than his usual contained self when she finally walked into the drawing-room.

'Do you normally wear a dinner jacket in the evenings?' she enquired, irritated at seeing him dressed formally.

'Tonight's special, don't you think?'

'No. But if you'd like me to change into a flowing ballgown, I'll be happy to oblige.'

'I can think of other ways you could be obliging.'

'You've got a one-track mind!'

'In that respect I'm no different from other men. Though you seem bloody determined to think I am.'

'Bloody?' she mocked. 'My, my, that's a strong word coming from you!'

'Keep provoking me,' he murmured, 'and I'll have an excuse to carry you upstairs and teach you a lesson.'

'You must be jo——' She didn't finish, for the sight of his mouth—thin with anger—warned her to watch her tongue. She was trying his patience and he was waiting for a chance to lose it.

'You're wearing your "I-hate-Randall" look,' he commented, coming across to her with a glass of champagne.

'You're quite wrong. I was wondering what other wifely duties you expect me to perform.'

'The usual ones. Hostessing my dinner parties, charming my friends and running my home on oiled wheels. Think you can manage?'

'Easily. But nothing more, Randall.'

'If you'd rather not share my suite,' he said unexpectedly, 'you can have the one at the end of the corridor.'

'Why the change of heart?'

'I don't want you thinking I'm pushing myself on you. I promised not to rush you.'

Wonders never ceased! For the second time in days Pearson the Paragon was climbing down. But funnily enough, now he had, Sandra appreciated his earlier point of view.

'I'm quite happy to remain where I am. We'll only be sharing the entrance foyer, as you said, and there's a good stout lock on my door.'

'Then why did you make such a song and dance?'

'I guess I over-reacted.'

'I can't think why.' He replenished his drink, pressing savagely down on the soda syphon. 'You're no innocent.'

He should only know! Swallowing the impulse to enlighten him, she preceded him into the dining-room, smaller than the one at Wideacres, 'small' being relative of course, for it could seat thirty people comfortably. The furniture wasn't as ponderous either, being French painted wood in soft apple green and rose.

'You have a marvellous cook,' she commented, halfway through the meal.

'I'm glad you think so. She uses a judicious mix of *nouvelle cuisine* and English.' Randall helped himself to more vegetables. 'I like to cut out fats and dairy produce wherever possible.'

'I didn't figure you for a health nut.'

'You think it nutty to look after one's body?'

She couldn't argue with this, nor did she want to, though it went against the grain to agree with him.

After dinner he retired to his study to work on a report, and she watched television before going to bed. She locked her door as she had said she would, feeling foolish as she did. In the glitzy atmosphere of a luxury hotel it hadn't been outlandish to envisage him pouncing on her like some villain in a melodrama, but in the discreet opulence of his home it seemed a figment of an overheated imagination. Pity the ring on her finger wasn't imagination too!

Next day Sandra spent with her father, setting the pattern for the rest of the month.

Only as March arrived did she find herself ready to spend more time at Oakland and take an interest in the running of the house. Wideacres reflected her father's character—large, rambling, imposing—and she wondered if Oakland mirrored Randall's. But that was impossible! She wouldn't feel as at home there if it did. But enough of him! For the moment this was her house too, and she would introduce her own personality into it.

'Would you mind if I made a few changes?' she asked him one Saturday afternoon as they sat together in the conservatory, enjoying what little sun there was.

'Do whatever you like,' he shrugged. 'It's your home as much as mine.'

'It isn't.'

'Let's compromise and say it's ours!' His look was long and measured. 'I've grown used to having you around, and wouldn't fancy living here alone again.'

'I doubt you'd have to. Half the ladies in the county would be clamouring to move in with you!'

'Yet you can't wait to move out!' Randall rose and wandered over to the massed bank of hyacinths lining the length of the glass wall. 'Do you really dislike being here with me?'

'Not as much as I thought I would,' she admitted.

He laughed. 'Thanks for such honesty. You're definitely your father's daughter!'

'I didn't realise how much until you showed me.'

'You've shown *me* a lot too,' he said.

'I can't imagine what.'

'Can't you?' He returned to his chair, took off his glasses and began polishing them. 'You've given me back my zest for living.'

'When I'm so awful to you most of the time?'

'It's the moments you aren't that count! You're like a hair shirt I enjoy wearing. You tease me when I'm pompous, provoke me when I least expect it, and generally make such a nuisance of yourself that I'm never bored with you.'

'That's a scorpion's compliment,' she sniffed. 'But despite the sting in the tail, I appreciate it.'

'I could say much nicer things.'

'I'd rather you didn't. You don't love me and it's silly pretending you do.'

He went on looking in her direction, though she knew he only saw her as a blur. Maybe that was what he preferred, for then he could imagine she was his lady love!

'There's one thing I'm curious to know, Randall. When you proposed to me all those years ago, were you already in love with that other woman?'

'My God!' he said despairingly. 'Can't you drop the subject?'

'I might if I met your dark lady of the sonnets! You should introduce me.'

He replaced his glasses, and with it the persona she recognised. 'She isn't dark. Her colouring's like yours.'

'I can dye my hair if it confuses you.'

'Shut up!' With unexpected violence Randall flung back his chair and strode aggressively to the door. 'Don't try my patience any further or I won't be responsible for my actions.'

He banged the door shut, leaving Sandra staring after him, nervous of the anger she had provoked, yet strangely elated by her ability to arouse it.

CHAPTER TEN

BEING a lady of leisure didn't appeal to Sandra. Yet finding a job locally to utilise her talent was well nigh impossible, and she was puzzling over how to occupy herself when Aileen telephoned to say she was back home and would Sandra come to tea?

Delighted to renew their acquaintance, Sandra went that very day. Aileen's home was a serene little Queen Anne house, its garden ablaze with flowers, its interior a delightful blend of the old and the modern—dark, gleaming furniture to offset her husband's brightly coloured paintings.

Aileen appeared somehow younger, in a fine wool dress of soft greens, above which her hair glowed like a flame.

'Bright, isn't it?' she laughed, noticing Sandra's eyes on it. 'You only saw it in the dimness of the hotel restaurant!'

'It's a glorious colour,' Sandra said.

'Dominic called it Titian, but Randall always teases me by calling it carroty.'

Once again Sandra was being shown another side of Randall. Was Aileen doing it deliberately to prove how little she herself knew him?

They had tea in the cosy sitting-room at the back of the house, after which Aileen showed her Dominic's studio, kept exactly as it was the day he had gone sailing.

'I suppose it's morbid of me still keeping the studio,' she murmured. 'One day I'll move house and pack the memories away.'

Would it be a move to Oakland? Sandra wondered. Randall had said he didn't want to live alone again, so what better for him eventually to turn to this warm and lovely woman?

Back in the sitting-room, Aileen went to a drawer in a walnut bureau and took out a manuscript, part story, part illustrations. 'The children's book Dominic was working on,' she explained.

Sandra leafed through it, pausing here and there to get the gist of the story, and noting how aptly the beautiful sketches depicted the adventures in the text.

'You simply *have* to publish it,' she exclaimed. 'It isn't only the children who'll love it, but everyone who admires your husband's work.'

'That's what the publishers keep telling me,' Aileen admitted. 'And I'd agree if they found an artist I approve of to finish it. But I don't like any of the samples they've sent me. Here, see for yourself.'

From another drawer she extracted some half-dozen watercolours and passed them across.

'Hmm, I see what you mean. They're not nearly good enough.'

'Fancy having a go at it yourself?' Aileen questioned, her expression not as casual as her voice, convincing Sandra she had been invited here for this very reason. Deeply touched, she none the less shook her head.

'I'm nowhere near good enough either.'

'Randall thinks you are—and I trust his judgement. He says the watercolours you did for your father's bedroom are exactly the style I'm looking for.'

Sandra was vaguely put out that Randall hadn't mentioned that he had spoken to Aileen since her return from California. It wasn't until this morning that she herself had known the woman was home.

'Do have a crack at it,' pressed Aileen. 'You've nothing to lose.'

'Except our friendship,' Sandra said drily, managing to hide her other feelings. 'If you don't like what I do you must promise to be honest with me.'

'You have my word on that. If this book isn't right, it won't appear.'

Sandra took the manuscript and drawings home, saying nothing about them to Randall, though she made no secret of having had tea with Aileen. Two could play at secrets, she thought crossly, and wondered if she would ever get to know this enigmatic man whose name she bore.

'Does Aileen have a job or is she fully occupied with her husband's exhibitions?' she asked him.

'You mean you were with her all afternoon and didn't ask her?' Randall was amused.

'We never got around to it.'

'She's a textile designer. One of the best.'

'She should get married again,' Sandra found herself saying.

'I agree.'

'She'd make an excellent wife for you, once we part!'

'I'll remember that.'

It was an answer Sandra hadn't expected, and she burned with resentment. Yet why was she so dog-in-the-manger? She shouldn't care a hoot what he did when she left him. Her attitude set her thinking of Barry. It was nearly two months since she had seen him, and she was curious to know what he was doing with his life. Not that it was hard to guess. The question was, with whom!

'They're interviewing the chairman of one of our rival companies on TV tonight,' Randall broke into her thoughts. 'Care to watch it?'

Nodding, she followed him to his study, a room she rarely came into, regarding it as Randall's private domain, and she sank into a leather armchair close to the log fire. Log fires were a feature of the house, and she had been surprised when the housekeeper had informed her Randall insisted on them, despite the modern central heating.

'I like the look of them and the smell of wood smoke,' he explained when she remarked on it now, and leaned forward to switch on the television before sinking into a wing chair. He was casual in fine wool pants and loose jacket of some silvery grey material, and she could visualise him in a few years, a little less lean and more relaxed, with a silver-blond boy on his knee—or a red-haired little girl perhaps?

'I don't think I'll watch TV after all,' she announced, jumping up. 'I've some telephone calls to make, so I'll say goodnight.'

She almost ran from the room, not knowing what she was running from, only that sitting with Randall had suddenly become stifling.

Next morning she read Dominic's manuscript from cover to cover, carefully studying each drawing and setting about doing a few more in a style which, though not emulating his, was not so rampantly different as to surprise the eye.

The whole of that day she worked in the conservatory, sketching and discarding, careful to clear away her things by five in case Randall came home early, for she did not want him to see what she was doing until she was sure she could do it well. She wished she knew if Aileen had told him she had agreed to tackle the illustrations, but had no intention of asking him. If he wanted to play his cards close to his chest concerning his friendship with the woman, let him!

She spent next day at the drawing board too, gratified when her brush flowed more freely, and pretty sure that she could handle the commission.

She was eyeing her last illustration with pleasure when she had the feeling of being watched and, swinging round, saw Randall behind her.

'You're home early,' she exclaimed. 'It's only four!'

'Your father's fine,' he said, quietening her obvious fear. 'I had a board meeting which finished sooner than expected, and decided to take advantage of it.' He bent to look at the sketch. 'Excellent. I'm glad you decided to do the book. I think this sort of work's your forte.'

'I'm afraid you're right,' Sandra admitted.

'Why afraid?'

'Well, when you dream of being another Berthe Morisot, you don't fancy being regarded as a modern-day Beatrix Potter!'

'How about a Sandra Pearson?'

'I prefer to use Sandra *Harris* for my work.'

'Like Wellington, you never miss an opportunity, do you?' he remarked.

'What?'

Randall's expression was wry. 'He had a weak bladder and never missed the opportunity of using a urinal if he saw one! In your case you never miss out on making a crack at me.'

'I'm sorry. I try not to, but ...'

'Forget it. What matters is that you don't go on wasting your talent.'

Aileen endorsed this when she saw Sandra's sketches.

'They're exactly what I want. I had a hunch you could do it.' She reached for her telephone. 'I'll call Howard Ellis—the publisher—and arrange to see him.'

'I don't need to go with you,' Sandra said hastily.

'You certainly do! He'll want to meet you.'

Two days later Sandra met the man who had made his reputation publishing the very best in children's books. He was as happy with the illustrations as Aileen, and by the time the two of them left his office, Sandra had a contract in her purse and an advance cheque in royalties.

'You're on the way to the top,' said Randall when she waved it in front of him later that evening.

She grinned. 'It might just buy me a dress and a half!'

'Only if you persist in having Lagerfeld originals!'

'Actually I'm putting the money into a special fund for a pet charity,' she replied.

'Pet as in animal, or pet as in something you're fond of?' he asked.

'Pet as in animal. Donkeys, actually. I've a soft spot for them.'

'Would it improve *our* relationship if I brayed at you?'

Sandra avoided his eyes. 'I'll have to work like a demon to get the drawings done,' she said as if he hadn't spoken. 'Mr Ellis wants to bring out the book for the autumn.'

'I'm glad you've got a tight deadline.'

'Why?'

'I'm looking forward to you doing a book of your own.'

'I wouldn't have a clue what to write about.'

'Donkeys?'

Sandra's mouth fell open. If she'd the sense she was born with, she'd have thought of it herself! She suddenly remembered the donkey she had been given as a child. 'Carrots' she had called him; an unoriginal name for a highly original animal with a will of its own.

'I might have a go at it,' she said aloud.

'Good. We'll fix you up a studio. Would you like to convert a room in the house, or have something built in the garden?'

'I'll think about it. Don't rush me, Randall. I'm not one of your business projects.'

'Sorry,' he said swiftly. 'I was only trying to help.'

'You enjoy being bossy, don't you?'

'I never think of myself like that. I simply enjoy organising. But my parents call me bossy too, so you may be right!' He hesitated momentarily. 'If they don't come back from Tasmania this year, we'll fly out to see them for Christmas. They'd only planned a three-month visit to my sister and her family, but once the twins arrived, they couldn't tear themselves away.'

'Wait till *you* have children,' she teased, then stopped, face flaming. Talk about donkeys, she was a prize one herself! She braced herself for Randall's rejoinder, and was amazed when none came.

Instead he switched on the television, saying casually, 'We've a new commercial I'd like to see.'

Sandra watched as 'Harris Pharmaceuticals' lit up the screen, and for the next sixty seconds saw the company itself—rather than a particular product—being extolled.

'Like it?' asked Randall.

'It's great for insomniacs!'

'That boring, eh? Can't say I disagree with you. I'm meeting our advertising agency in London on Monday to discuss it.' He lowered the sound with the remote control. 'I'm staying the night and I'd like you to come with me.'

'I won't disappear while you're gone!'

'That's not why I asked you. But I've a business dinner with the Managing Director of our German subsidiary who's coming over with his wife, and it would let me off the hook if you could entertain her.'

'That's what wives are for,' Sandra said flippantly.

'And for other things too,' came the murmur.

Her heart pounded heavily, but she managed to look unconcerned, watching the television programme as if it was the most interesting she'd ever seen.

The evening passed as usual. Randall disappeared into his study, and though she had made a habit of wandering in to sit with him the last few weeks, tonight she was too edgy to do so.

He was still working when she finally went to her room, and she didn't bother interrupting him to say goodnight; they didn't have that sort of relationship. Nor did she ever breakfast with him, though she was an early riser, for there was an intimacy in sharing coffee and toast and the morning papers which she shied away from, always making certain Randall had left the house before she went downstairs.

Next morning she was buttering a croissant when he called her from the office to say he had left some papers in the drawer of his bedside table, and would she give them to the chauffeur who was on his way back for them?

'You're not normally forgetful,' she chided.

'I worked till three last night, and couldn't think straight this morning,' he explained.

'I'll have them ready,' she promised, and hurried upstairs.

Though they shared the same suite, she had never been into his room, and she found it almost identical to hers, except the colour scheme was tan and cream instead of blue and white. Averting her eyes from the bed, she opened the drawer of the bedside table. She couldn't see any papers—only a couple of books—and was about to shut the drawer when something at the back of it caught her eye. The papers Randall wanted had crumpled up on themselves, and she carefully pulled them out, bringing with them a small suede box.

Memory stirred and she remembered Randall's proposal and his present to her on the night of her eighteenth birthday. Slowly opening the box, her memory was confirmed as she saw the delicate, hand-painted miniature.

She knew he had taken it back, but was amazed he had kept it. It could hardly be from sentiment, considering how rude she had been to him! So what reason was there? But Randall's actions frequently puzzled her, and it was pointless speculating.

Carefully replacing the box, she went downstairs with the documents, sealed them in an envelope and left them on the hall table ready for the chauffeur.

That night over dinner she casually mentioned that she had discovered the miniature, and asked Randall why he had kept it.

'It's a collector's item,' he answered without inflection.

'I never knew you collected lockets.'

'There are many things you don't know about me.'

'You enjoy being mysterious, don't you?'

'It's one way of holding a woman's interest! If a man's an open book they find him boring.'

'There's a happy medium,' she grumbled. 'You're a book with all the pages stuck together!'

He set down his knife and fork and looked directly at her. 'What would you like to know about me?'

She nearly blurted out, 'How you feel about your lady love?' but refused to give him the satisfaction. 'Nothing,' she said aloud. 'I know as much about you as I want.'

He resumed eating. 'You haven't forgotten you're coming with me to London tomorrow? We're staying overnight at the Connaught, and I suggest you have dinner there with Mrs Schwartz, rather than take her out.'

'Whatever you say.'

He half smiled. 'It's for the good of the company. And as you're one of the major shareholders...'

'If I weren't, you wouldn't have married me!' she snapped.

Their glances clashed across the table, and they finished the meal in silence.

They left for London early next morning, Randall at the wheel and seeming in fine humour. 'It's unusual being alone with you,' he remarked as they cruised along the motorway.

'We're mostly alone.'

'In a house full of servants who'd come running if you screamed?'

A quick glance in his direction showed her he was teasing, and she relaxed.

He was quick to sense it and gave her one of his rare smiles. 'Given any more thought to Carrots?'

She was momentarily puzzled. 'It's not a vegetable I'm particularly fond of.'

'The donkey,' he chuckled, 'not the vegetable!'

'Oh, *Carrots*,' she laughed. 'No. I couldn't work up any enthusiasm. I've an idea about a snow leopard, though.'

'Intriguing creatures. If they get any rarer they'll become almost mythological. You look a bit like a cat yourself with your tawny gold hair and eyes.'

'And you're like a snow leopard,' she said impulsively. 'You have the same aura of strength and stealth.'

'I'm not sure I like that.' He slowed speed to look at her. 'Do you always relate people to animals?'

'Do you?' she countered. 'You likened me to one first.'

'I suppose I do,' he said reflectively.

'How do you see Aileen?'

'As a poodle. Decorative, yet extremely capable.'

'What about the woman you love?' she asked.

'Aah, I should have known you'd get on to her!'

'Don't answer if you'd rather not,' Sandra said in a 'I-couldn't-care-less' voice.

'But I want to. In looks she's catlike—like you. But in character she's a palomino. Aristocratic, high-spirited, and responding to a firm hand!'

'But eventually not yours.'

'Too true.' As if the acknowledgement had soured him, Randall lapsed into silence for the rest of the journey.

It was noon when they reached their two-bedroom suite at the Connaught and found several messages waiting for them on the entrance hall table.

'Looks as if I won't be lunching with you,' he said, frowning down at one of the messages in his hand.

'I wasn't expecting you to. I'm having lunch with a couple of girls from art school.'

The quick lift of his eyebrow showed disbelief—he probably suspected she was meeting Barry—and for an instant Sandra was sorry she wasn't. That would certainly have given Randall something unpalatable to chew on! But not even the thought of annoying him would have prompted her to contact the man who had let her down so badly.

'May I drop you anywhere?' he asked. 'I'm taking a cab to the Savoy.'

'That's hardly en route to Baker Street,' she answered blandly. 'Pity, really. I could have introduced you to my friends.'

Not by a flicker of a lash did he show he knew she was getting at him.

'At least we can share the lift,' she added.

'By all means.'

It was full when they entered it, and Sandra saw two young women eye Randall with evident interest. Seeing him through their eyes she had to concede he was worth looking at, his dark suit a foil for his silvery fair hair, his gold-framed glasses giving his face an ascetic quality at variance with the sensual curve of his mouth, while his aloof air was not borne out by the whipcord strength of a body that his excellently cut suit emphasised.

I wonder what he's like in bed? The thought came unheralded and jolted her, making her recall his assertion that he wouldn't be satisfied with a platonic marriage for long. Almost as though reading her mind—and where she was concerned he always seemed to—he edged closer to her. She held her breath, not wishing to absorb the scent of him, and admitting with dismay that if he and ten other men were alone with her in an unlighted room, she would know instantly which one was Randall.

The doors slid back at the ground floor, and she almost fell out in her eagerness to put some space between them.

'I'll see you here later, then,' he said, waiting outside with her while the commissionaire hailed her a cab.

Nodding, Sandra dived in, breathing a sigh of relief as the taxi pulled away from the kerb.

For the next few hours she was too absorbed to give any thought to Randall. It was a year since she had seen Ann Daintry and her twin sister Mercia, for they had accepted a job in Italy immediately after graduating, and had returned only six weeks ago.

'We couldn't believe it when we heard you were married,' Ann said as Sandra walked into the large studio that took up the top floor of a narrow Georgian house a stone's throw from Harley Street. 'The last time you wrote us you were raving about someone called Barry.'

'A temporary aberration,' Sandra said nonchalantly. 'Randall's worth ten of him.'

'Talking of ten,' Mercia's gamin face was alight with mischief, 'how does he rate on the scale?'

Sandra grinned. 'There are some things one doesn't even discuss with one's closest friends!'

She strolled over to the artists' table, amazed to see a beautiful series of animal drawings: tigers, lions, panthers and—wonder of wonders—snow leopards!

'Do you have a reference book for these?' she asked, tapping the snow leopard with her finger. 'I'm thinking of doing a children's story about one.'

Ann instantly went to a cupboard and took out a tattered magazine. 'You can borrow this as long as you let us have it back. It's got the most sensational photographs.'

Gratefully Sandra took it, feeling as though she had been given a divine nudge.

'Are you writing the story or only illustrating it?'

'Both—I hope. And I'll guard this magazine with my life!'

It was four o'clock when Sandra left her friends, having shared gossip and French bread and cheese, washed down with a bottle of wine which added a spring to her step as she headed down Baker Street to the Connaught.

'I don't believe it!' an all too familiar male voice said as a taxi screeched to a halt beside her and Barry descended from it.

Sandra stopped as if poleaxed.

'Not five minutes ago I was thinking of you,' he went on, catching her arm. 'I thought you were still buried in the country.'

'I came up to town with my husband.' Her heart was hammering so loudly she could barely hear herself speak. 'I—I'll take this cab if you're finished with it, Barry— I'm in a hurry.'

'Hey, I'm not letting you go like this—we've got to talk.'

'We've nothing to say.' She opened the cab door.

'We've plenty to say.' He climbed in after her. 'You look great, Sandra. More beautiful than I remember.'

'Marriage agrees with me.' Let him digest that one!

'So it appears.' Barry's glance was speculative. 'Your husband wasn't quite the local yokel I thought.'

'That should teach you not to jump to conclusions.'

'Particularly where you're concerned. Was it love on his side too,' Barry continued waspishly, 'or did he see you as the boss's daughter?'

'Darling Barry,' she cooed, 'always the gallant!'

'I like calling a spade a spade. The one thing in my favour is that I never sucked up to you when you told me who you were.'

True, and trust Barry to ram it home. If only she hadn't bumped into him! His skin was bronzer, his hair seemed blacker and shone like satin, and there was a vibrant air about him in direct contrast to Randall's quiet calm.

She found herself trembling and was aware that Barry knew his effect on her. She tried to distance herself mentally, to study him as if he were a stranger sharing her cab rather than the man who might once have shared her life.

'What's with you these days?' she managed to ask.

'Work and play, in that order.' He edged closer. 'I have to see you, Sandra. Are you free for dinner tonight?'

'I didn't know married women were your scene!'

'They're not, but *you* are. God, if you knew how much I regret my stupidity! You were the best thing in my life and I let you go.'

Pity he hadn't said this months ago. Sandra was filled with a bitterness she couldn't hide. 'I'm married, Barry, and I don't play around.'

'I'm not asking you to. I just want to talk to you.'

'Talk, then.'

'Alone. You know what I mean.'

'I'm not sure I do.' She pushed back a damp lock of hair from her forehead. 'I love my husband, and I don't see the point in our meeting.'

'Not even as friends?'

'I don't think of you as a friend. And whatever there was between us is dead.'

'Not as far as I'm concerned. I actually dialled your number the day before your wedding, but got cold feet and hung up.'

Thank heavens he had! She couldn't even begin to think how she would have reacted had he not. But it was the last thing she would ever admit to him, and forced herself to say contemptuously, 'I'm glad you did, Barry. There's nothing more dead than a dead love.'

'I agree. Except that our love isn't dead. Despite what you say, you still feel something for me. I can read it in your face.'

'Then you must be dyslexic!' she rejoined, and breathed a sigh of relief as she saw the Connaught ahead of her. Even as the cab slowed, she opened the door and jumped out.

'We can't part like this,' Barry followed her. 'At least say you forgive me and have a drink with me.'

'I forgive you without the drink,' Sandra said promptly and, before he could stop her, pushed past him into the hotel, heart pounding, body trembling, brain too numbed to feel anything.

CHAPTER ELEVEN

SANDRA could not get Barry out of her mind. What a shock it had been seeing him again. Only a shock? Surprisingly yes, and she found it hard to understand. Unless she had put her love for him into cold storage and it had frozen so hard it needed time to melt?

But would meeting him again serve any purpose? It was probably wiser not to re-open the wound. She was managing to cope with her life, so why court trouble? Because Barry *was* trouble. If she saw him again her defences might crumble and the situation become dangerously untenable. There was also the fear of Randall finding out. Fond though he was of her father, and ambitious for himself, he wouldn't tolerate being cuckolded.

Reaching their suite, she bathed and donned an elegant black crêpe dress, the fitted bodice drawing attention to her high, full breasts and tiny waist, the wide skirt standing out from below the hips almost like a peplum. Not quite the garb for dining with a middle-aged small-town lady, and one that would certainly raise Randall's eyebrows. But what the hell! Meeting Barry had unsettled her, and this high fashion was her armour plating!

She was brushing her tawny gold hair when she heard the outer door close. Hurriedly spraying herself with *Arpège*, she went into the sitting-room. There was no sign of Randall and she wandered around aimlessly, pausing by the window to look out at the steady stream of rush-hour traffic.

She glanced at her watch. Seven o'clock. She had no idea when Mrs Schwartz would be arriving, and didn't fancy being cooped up with Randall in a hotel suite; it smacked of an intimacy that unsteadied her.

Impatiently she knocked on his door and at his 'Come in', did so. He was standing by the bureau, glasses off, tying the sash of a wine silk dressing-gown which parted as he swung around to her, giving her a glimpse of a long, muscular leg.

'How was your day?' he asked.

'Fine.' She remained firmly by the door. 'How was yours?'

'Long. Did you see your friends?'

Checking up on her, was he? Sandra ignored the question. 'What time am I meeting Mrs Schwartz?'

'Eight. You still have an hour.'

She turned to leave, and he called, 'Stay and talk to me.'

'Come into the sitting-room and I will.'

'Scared to talk in here?' He moved towards her and knocked into a table. 'Blast! Where are my glasses?'

He looked myopically around, but Sandra's keen glance spied them glinting at the foot of the bed, and she retrieved them for him before returning to the sitting-room.

He joined her a few moments later, his silent air of leashed strength once more reminding her of a snow leopard. A germ of a story sprouted in her mind and she smiled.

'What's amusing you?' asked Randall.

'My snow leopard's springing to life.'

'That's great.' The pleasure on his face took years off him, giving her a picture of how he might have looked at twenty.

'Have you always worn glasses?' she asked impulsively.

'Since I was ten. My father wears them too.'

'They say short-sightedness runs in families.'

'I hope it skips ours,' he said. 'Wearing glasses has been the bane of my life.'

'Have you never tried contact lenses?'

'I did for a while, but my eyes were too sensitive for hard lenses and soft ones don't take to accurate prescriptions. Anyway, I regard them as more of a cosmetic need—something our daughters might have to concern themselves with.'

At this second reference to a family it was an effort for Sandra to appear calm.

'No comment?' Randall questioned. 'You can't always distance yourself when our conversation hits a nerve.'

'I haven't.' She essayed a smile. 'I'm still here, aren't I?'

'But surrounded by a mental wall.'

'What do you expect me to say? We've got a phoney marriage and I won't add to it by phoney talk.'

'Phoney is one thing it isn't,' he stated. 'I'm serious about wanting a family and serious about not waiting too long.'

'How can you even *consider* bringing children into a marriage that's meaningless?' she cried.

'It won't be meaningless once we *have* a family!'

Panic caught her and she jumped up.

'What's it to be?' he went on conversationally. 'Fight or flight?'

'I'm in no position to fight and I can't take flight. For the moment I'm your prisoner.'

'What a harsh way of seeing it! And may I remind you it's a prison of your own making?' He sat down and nonchalantly crossed one leg over the other. 'Try to think of our marriage positively. You may find you don't dislike me as much as you think.'

'You promised not to rush me,' she said raggedly.

'I've been your husband nearly three months.'

'That's no time at all!'

'I'm not saying we should have a child right away, but we should at least start thinking in terms of a real marriage. I want us to get to know each other. I want to learn and understand your body as well as your mind, and I want you to do the same with me.'

He was practically quoting Mario! She put shaky hands to her head, disarraying the fashionable curls. Even when she had loved Barry she had found it impossible to give in to him, so how much more difficult would it be with a man who meant nothing to her?

Through the tangle of her lashes she glanced at him, wondering what he would say if she told him about Mario. Would he be sympathetic or dismiss her fears as childish? No, she could never tell him.

'I can't do as you ask,' she said huskily. 'I can't make love to a man when I know he wants someone else.'

The telephone forestalled his reply, and he rose to answer it.

Sandra breathed a sigh of relief. She had every reason to feel edgy with him in a hotel, and the sooner they returned to Oakland the better.

'The Schwartzes are downstairs,' he told her, replacing the receiver.

Hurriedly Sandra picked up her bag and went into the lobby, so intent on escape that she was at the elevator before he had closed the door of their suite.

'We'll continue our discussion at a more auspicious time,' he said, joining her.

Not if *I* have any say in the matter, she thought, yet knew her father's frail health kept her firmly in the prison she had made for herself.

The Schwartzes were waiting for them in the bar, and Sandra found herself warming to the woman whose softly coiffed grey hair and stylish dress proved that, provincial or not, fashion today was universal. Physically she was twice the size of her husband—a dapper little man with a shock of black hair, whose forceful manner was in direct contrast to Randall's.

The two men left to dine at Randall's club, and Sandra led Mrs Schwartz into the dining-room. As always it was crowded and the food excellent, and after two glasses of vintage hock, Mrs Schwartz needed little encouragement to chat happily away about her children and grandchildren.

By the time they reached the coffee stage, Sandra could itemise every minor ailment the woman's grandchildren had suffered, and she was debating whether to plead a headache and retire early when she was astonished to see Barry wending his way towards them.

'Hi, Sandra,' he greeted her, 'mind if I join you for coffee?'

Short of being rude she couldn't refuse, so she nodded, and stiffly introduced him to her guest. With his usual aplomb he soon took over the conversation, and charmed Mrs Schwartz. But then who wouldn't be beguilded by a dark-eyed Romeo who treated you with the warmth he might have bestowed on a much younger woman?

Sandra sat back, letting him have the field. It was quite a while since she had been a spectator to Barry's game play, and she was surprised to find it no longer amused her, seeing it not only as an act to impress but as an integral part of his character. Barry never wasted his charm needlessly, and she wondered cynically what he hoped to gain from Mrs Schwartz, or maybe he was showing herself what she was missing by rejecting him?

Distance hadn't lent him enchantment, she decided, watching his phoney smile and the movements of his broad-chested body. He had gained weight these past months, or did he look fatter because she was accustomed to Randall's leanness?

Perhaps it was because of Randall that she was also more critical of Barry, for marrying him had matured her, opening up new avenues of her mind and giving her a broader perspective on life. The headstrong girl who had hankered after Barry had disappeared, and the girl she now was would never be taken in by him again. He meant nothing to her. Absolutely nothing!

I'm free of him! she realised, and wanted to sing and shout with the joy of it.

'We'd best be going,' Barry said suddenly, looking at her.

'Where?'

'To Janet's.' He flashed Mrs Schwartz one of his winning smiles. 'I hope you don't mind if I take Sandra away from you, but a friend of ours is moving to California and is throwing a farewell party.'

'Of course I don't mind,' Mrs Schwartz smiled back.

'I'm not going to any party,' Sandra stated.

'Come on, darling,' chuckled Barry, 'Mrs Schwartz says it's OK, and Janet will be disappointed not to see you.'

Short of a public row with him, she could not argue, so she gave in, though the instant her guest was wafted up in the lift to her room, she rounded on Barry in a fury.

'How dare you force yourself on me like this?'

'I'm doing you a favour—or were you enjoying your tête-à-tête with Mrs Dullsville?'

'Much as it may surprise you, I was. Now if you don't mind...' Sandra pushed past him and headed for the stairs, preferring to climb the two flights than be with him a moment longer.

'Have a heart, Sandra!' Barry stepped ahead of her and barred her way.

'I have,' she snapped, 'and it belongs to my husband! Now goodnight, Barry. I'm going to no party with you.'

'There isn't one—I invented it to get you alone. But if you don't trust yourself with me...'

She laughed, once more overwhelmed by her new-found freedom. 'You mean nothing to me, Barry. Can't you get that into your conceited head?'

'I'd believe you if you didn't run away from me.'

She sighed. 'OK, I'll have a drink with you.' She turned and led the way to the bar, disconcerted when he caught her arm and stopped her.

'Not here, sweetheart. I prefer neutral territory.'

Expecting him to take her to a quiet wine bar where they could 'talk'—as he had put it—Sandra was irritated to find herself in a noisy Mayfair disco, where he seemed content to entertain her with the latest agency gossip: who had left, who was climbing the corporate ladder, who was sliding down it. Not him, of course—he was several rungs higher since she had worked there, and seemed set to get to the top.

Despite herself, she was interested in what he said, and idly wondered what the future would have held for her had she gone to live with him. It definitely wouldn't have worked. Sooner or later she'd have seen what a self-centred egoist he was. Heck, they'd been together an hour and he hadn't even asked how her father was!

She pushed back her chair. 'I've had a long day, Barry. If you want to stay on, I'll take a cab.'

'Don't be silly. I'll drive you.'

Within moments they were on their way, but instead of heading towards the hotel, he drew into a cul-de-sac off Grosvenor Square.

'If only I'd had the sense to know what I was losing,' he began huskily. 'I love you, Sandra, and want to marry you.'

She almost laughed in his face. 'I'm already married, or have you forgotten? And even if I wasn't——'

'Don't,' he cut in, pulling her into his arms and ig-noring her struggles as he went to kiss her.

Infuriated, Sandra tried to push him away, but the action fired him to a greater show of strength and his hold grew brutal.

'Don't turn away from me, Sandra. I meant what I said.'

'So did I,' she said flatly, knowing that any further show of anger might inflame him all the more. 'Please take me to the hotel. It's late and I'm tired.'

For answer his grip firmed, and to show she meant what she said, she tried to reach for the door handle.

'Why the rush?' muttered Barry.

Ignoring him, she struggled to free herself, but the movement of her body excited him further, and his moist breath was raucous in her ear, as were his unintelligible mutterings of desire.

With superhuman strength she freed her leg from the weight of his thigh and dug her heel viciously into his foot. With an expletive he pulled back, and seizing her chance she opened the door and jumped out. But her dash for freedom was impeded by her high heels, and she had hardly gone five yards when he caught her and pulled her to a stop.

'Let me go!' she screamed. 'Let me go!'

'Stop it!' he cried, shading her hard. 'I won't harm you. I just don't want us to part enemies.'

'We sure as hell won't part friends!'

'Don't say that.' His fingers dug into her arms, and recognising his superior strength, Sandra went limp.

'That's better,' he grunted. 'Now listen to me. First I want to apologise. I misjudged the situation and acted like a fool.'

'You can say that again!'

'But you can't blame me. Not long ago you said you loved me, and I couldn't believe you'd changed so soon. But if you have, I accept it, though I hope we can be friends.'

It was the last thing she could envisage, but having given his ego one blow, she decided not to administer another.

'Of course we'll be friends,' she said lightly, and hiding her trepidation, returned with him to the car.

As if to prove she could trust him, Barry behaved impeccably, keeping up a flow of small talk until he drew into the kerb outside the hotel entrance.

'One question only,' he said, leaning back in his seat. 'Did you marry on the rebound or for love?'

Aha! So he still had doubts. Well, she would scotch them once and for all. 'For love,' she said firmly. 'I've known Randall for years and took him for granted until my father had his heart attack. Then I realised how much I depended on him, and from there it was a short step to love.'

'I hope he knows what a lucky man he is,' Barry said heavily. 'I'd like to meet him some time.'

'I'll give you a call when we're next in London,' she lied.

'I've got a new account in Norfolk,' he disconcerted her by saying. 'Would you throw me out if I came to see you?'

'*I* won't,' she joked, 'but Randall might!'

'What does he know about me?'

'Enough not to lose any sleepless nights!'

'Ouch!' grunted Barry as he accompanied her up the steps. 'You hit hard.'

'Sorry,' she said saccharinely, and with a soft 'goodnight' disappeared into the lobby.

She found their suite in darkness and wondered if Randall was back. Hoping he wasn't and that she would be spared the necessity of explaining where she had been, she tiptoed to her room, and was on the threshold when she heard his door open. Turning, she saw his pyjamaed figure silhouetted against his bedside light.

'Where the hell have you been?' he demanded.

'I beg your pardon?'

'So you should, having made an utter fool of me!' He grabbed her arm and pulled her into his room, slamming the door behind them with his foot.

'Couldn't wait to see your boyfriend, could you? I should have guessed you'd planned this when you so readily agreed to come to London with me.'

'I made no plans to see him,' Sandra assured him.

'You mean he just happened to stroll into the Connaught tonight?'

'He knew I was here because we—we bumped into each other this afternoon.'

'Bumped into him?' sneered Randall. 'What a coincidence!'

'It's true! And I also told him I didn't want to see him again.'

'Which was why he came looking for you tonight? I know I've been an idiot where you're concerned, but I'm not idiot enough to swallow *that*. You encouraged him.'

'I didn't!'

'Then why did you go off with him and leave Mrs Schwartz?' How do you think I felt when Hans and I got back and she told me you'd gone out on a date?'

'I only went because Barry trumped up some story about a farewell party, and short of making a scene... Oh, can't you see that?'

'I see a lot of things,' Randall said thickly, 'and I don't like any of them!'

'For heaven's sake credit me with some intelligence!' she said vehemently. 'If I'd wanted to see Barry, I wouldn't have done it so blatantly.'

'Wouldn't you? Since when have you shown any concern for my finer feelings?'

Aware of the truth of this, she tried to defend herself.

'I know I've been bitchy to you in private, but never in public. We made a contract and I'll stand by it till the end.'

'There won't be an end,' he said with quiet menace. 'You agreed to be my wife, and my wife you'll remain—in *every* way.'

Sandra's scalp prickled. 'I think we should talk about it in the morning.'

'No more talk,' he said thickly. 'I've given you so much rope that you've started trussing *me* with it!'

Her fear increased, but she fought it down. 'You can't go back on your word. You agreed to give me time.'

'To have it off with another man? From now on any favours you give are to me!'

With an iron hand Randall dragged her from the door, and her feet slithered across the carpet as she tried to resist him. But she was no match for his strength, and he flung her across the bed and pinioned her there with his hands.

'As of now *I* call the shots,' he grated, staring down at her.

Mutely she glared into his face, a small part of her wryly acknowledging that no one could call this the most boring night of her life! First she had fought for her honour with Barry, now she would be doing it with Randall!

'Please,' she said in the gentlest possible tone, 'why are you so angry? Surely there's nothing wrong in having a drink with another man?'

'No newly married woman goes on seeing her ex-lover,' Randall bit out.

'He wasn't my lover!'

'Liar!'

'You're a fine one to talk!' Her temper began to fray. 'You lied about loving me when you asked me to marry you four years ago. At least *my* past's an open book.'

'Open to all and sundry,' he flared, his fingers sinking deeper into her shoulders. 'But from now on I'm the only one who'll be reading it!'

'Stop playing the heavy-handed husband with me!'

'I'm not playing. The games are over.'

Fear spiralled through her and, abandoning all pretence at calm, she tried to wrench free of him, digging her nails viciously into his hands in her effort to prize them off her. Randall grunted with pain and she delighted in it. But his grip remained viselike, and she went for him again, aware of drawing blood.

'Bitch!' His hands dropped from her and instantly Sandra rolled over and slithered to the far side of the bed. But he lunged at her and pulled her roughly back, flinging his body upon her and holding her captive with his weight.

'Don't fight me,' he grated. 'You're mine and I mean to have you.'

'Not like this you won't!' She pummelled at him with all her strength. 'I'll see you in hell first!'

'Then I'll take you with me!'

He tore at her dress, roughly yanking the zip, and she cried out in pain as it caught her skin. Uncaring, he ripped the fabric from her shoulders, revealing her honey satin bra and panties. 'How beautiful you are,' he said deep in his throat. 'Beautiful and untrustworthy—acting the ice maiden with me but giving yourself to a young pup who isn't fit to lick your shoes!'

'Barry wasn't my lover,' she cried, then made a consummate effort to placate him. She'd done practically the same with Barry less than an hour ago, and she knew that this time she was in greater danger, for though Randall was in command of himself, she knew she was on the edge of a precipice.

'I understand why you're angry with me,' she whispered in a little-girl voice. 'I know I haven't been the wife you wanted, but I swear I've never given myself to *any* man.' In a gesture too swift for him to stop, she reached up and took off his glasses, hoping that if she looked directly into his eyes, she could make him believe her. 'I'm a virgin, Randall. I swear it.'

'At twenty-two and beautiful as a siren? You don't honestly think I'll swallow that, do you?'

'It's true,' she reiterated. 'You see, when I was——'

She got no further, her words stifled by the fierceness of his mouth on hers.

Of such stuff were nightmares made, and the fears that had lain dormant in her mind rose to fill her with terror. She struggled like a mad thing, but she was a moth in a gale, battered down by a force so violent that she was powerless.

Randall was deaf to her cries, inflamed by desire and blind to reason. Yet it was not in her nature to give in, and she continued struggling, kicking at him, raking her nails across his skin.

'You'll never have me!' she vowed silently.

But the words were empty and she knew it, for his hands were everywhere, searching out the inner reaches of her body, leaving no curve untouched, no erotic pathway unkissed. Her skin was damp from the moisture of his tongue, her nipples throbbing peaks of red, the softness of her belly trembling as his head lowered to the silken skin, his mouth tracing a fiery path.

'No!' she cried. 'No!'

But her anguish spurred him on, and his tongue darted forward to an even greater intimacy.

In a mad rage she flailed out at him, and like a cobra he rose above her and wrenched her arms down to her sides. His breath was a hiss, his eyes glazed, his hair a damp fall of silver. He was no longer the Randall she knew, and to him she was no longer Sandra, but an unknown female on whom he could wreak his disillusionment and frustration.

In the wildness of their battle his pyjamas had long since been discarded, and the radiance of the nearby lamp gave his body a pearly quality, showing the muscles rippling beneath the surface and the fine scattering of dark blond hair across his breastbone. Sandra closed her eyes, though the throbbing against her inner thigh told her what she was afraid to look at.

Randall had no such inhibitions where she was concerned, and his silvery glance swept over her, a hungry searching that devoured her with its intensity. Naked she lay before him, hands pinned to her sides so she could not use them for cover. Defiantly she glared at him, and his rage dropped away, leaving only desire.

As if in slow motion, his face lowered to hers, looking younger now it was suffused with colour. His eyes were no longer opaque grey chips but diamonds of light gleaming from a fringe of baby-soft lashes. Then his mouth touched hers again and she was disarmed by the tenderness of his tongue as it snaked across her lips, the sinuous movement echoed by his hands on her breasts. Slowly and inexorably they aroused her, and desperately she fought to contain it, forcing her eyes open in the hope that keeping him in focus would keep at bay the tide of passion threatening to sweep over her.

What a false hope it was! For his hands set her alight as they moved from her breasts to the swell of her belly, then lower still to the curly mound of tawny hair.

He groaned and the pressure of his hips intensified as the swelling between his thighs nestled between hers, rubbing upon the soft inner skin.

Oh, God! Here was the intimacy she had long dreaded and never expected to happen. And certainly not with Randall! He was the last man in the world she had envisaged as her lover, and he soon *would* be unless she stopped him!

Stopped him? The very word was a joke when her body ached for his, silently urging those magic fingers never to cease their play, to go on for ever vibrating upon her, inside her. Tentatively her own hands ranged over him, fluttering across his shoulders to trace a delicate path down his spine, and then over the firm buttocks to the ridged muscles of his thighs.

Reading capitulation in her touch, he lifted his mouth from hers and lowered it to her nipples, sucking at them until she arched in a frenzy of yearning.

His breath on her silky hair and his tongue on her moist inner lips made her stiffen momentarily; then she was flooded with warmth, and parting her legs, invited him into the most intimate recesses of her being.

With a deep, satisfied sigh, he slid into her, giving a jerk of surprise as he felt the resistance of her virginity.

One cry from her, one moan, and she knew he would draw back. But a coupling that had begun in fury had turned for her into a pulsating, vibrating need that had to be assuaged. If it wasn't, she would scream, cry, die with longing.

Her legs parted wider still, and her hands pressed hard on his buttocks, pushing him into her with all her might. The speed of his entry made the pain of it so momentary that it was instantly swamped by the incredible, exhilarating feel of him inside her.

She shuddered with the intensity of her desire, caught in a spiral of passion that whirled her round and round until she was dizzy with longing. Clutching at his shoulder, she sobbed her need of him, twining her legs around his and aware of the increasing surge of him as her movements excited him further. Higher and deeper he plunged, caught in a frenzy he could not contain, taking her with him into a spinning vortex of white-hot sensation. Lost in him, she clung to him, and they were two parts of a whole, exploding in a simultaneous burst of ecstasy that made Randall shout with triumph, and Sandra cry with joy as he flooded himself into her.

A long while later, or was it only seconds—for what was time when reason was surrendered?—Sandra lay peacefully beside him, his quiet, even breathing proclaiming sleep; not the sleep of the just, she thought wryly, for though his taking of her had ended with a mutual climax of need, she could not forget it had begun with a violence that had been almost akin to rape. Indeed if she had gone on fighting him, it could well have been!

She waited to feel anger, but none came. I must be too exhausted, she thought sleepily, and sat up to go to her bedroom. But even in sleep, Randall felt her movement, and his outflung arm—resting lightly across her stomach—tightened its hold on her. Afraid that if she awakened him, he might take her again, she eased back on the pillow. One dramatic love scene a night was more than enough for her, before laying herself open to another. There was so much she had to think about, many crazy thoughts to still, but not now. She was in too 'high' a state to assess all that happened and what it meant to her. In the morning, after a night's sleep, she'd be able to cope with the situation and clear the air between herself and Randall.

With a half-sigh she closed her eyes and sank into oblivion.

CHAPTER TWELVE

SANDRA'S eyes fluttered open and rested on the empty pillow beside her. Memory flooded back and she sat up quickly, looking for Randall. But the suite was quiet as Juliet's tomb and, throwing aside the coverlet, she wrapped the sheet around her and padded into the sitting-room.

There was no sign of him here either, and with an odd sense of loss she realised he had gone out. She glanced round for a note, but seeing none returned to his room to

collect her clothing still scattered on the floor. As she gathered them up her cheeks burned, and she relived the night they had shared, finding it incredible that something begun in cold fury had ended in such ecstasy for her.

But why had he left without waking her, as though this morning was no different from any other? He was treating her like a one-night stand!

The telephone rang and she snatched at it.

'Hope I didn't wake you?'

The familiar voice set her heart pounding in a way that wasn't familiar at all. 'N-no, I was about to take a shower.'

'I'm afraid I left your bathroom in a bit of a mess. I used yours instead of mine so as not to disturb you.'

'Very thoughtful of you.' She meant it, but it came out mockingly.

'I can be,' Randall said quietly.

'What?'

'Thoughtful.'

'Oh.' What was the matter with her? Couldn't she be more scintillating? Yet there was so much to be said she didn't know where to begin, or maybe she was scared to begin because she didn't know where it would end. But that didn't make sense. Not surprising, for nothing was making sense, least of all the emotions he had aroused in her. But then it wasn't every day that she fought a man like a wildcat and then capitulated like a kitten! Yet it had been so sweet ... Stop it! she admonished herself. You're crazy!

'You still there?' Randall cut across her chaotic thoughts, bringing her back to a semblance of sanity.

'Yes! Why—why are you speaking so softly? Are you at a meeting?'

'Good guess. And it's likely to go on till this afternoon.'

'I'll do some shopping,' she said inconsequentially.

'Fine.' He paused. 'We must talk—you know that.'

'I know.' There she went again, doing a great imitation of a parrot.

'I should be back around four,' he went on. 'Do you want to stay the night or go home?'

'Whatever you like.'

'How dutiful of you!' He sounded amused.

'Sometimes it's better to be.'

There was a pregnant silence.

'We should have spoken before I left this morning,' he said. 'I—sorry, I must go. See you later.'

Alone with the purring receiver, Sandra set it on its rest and went into her bathroom. She picked up Randall's towel from the floor. It was still damp from his body and she clutched it to her breast, only conscious of doing so when she saw herself in the mirrored wall. She must be out of her tiny mind standing here with his towel like a lovesick idiot. But that was what she'd been for far too long; though stupidly it had been over Barry!

But he was in the past and she was finally free of him—
as she was free of Mario.

Free of Mario? She sank on to the edge of the bath.
Was it true? Had memory of him ceased to hurt her?
She waited for the loathing his name always engendered,
but felt nothing. She tested herself—bringing his face to
mind, his voice, the touch of his hands—but her pulse
remained steady, her body calm, and she knew that the
handsome Italian whose onslaught on her had haunted
her for years had finally faded into oblivion.

She was free of him, and Barry too. Only Randall had
to be removed from her life, and one day that would
also happen. Then why wasn't she jumping for joy?
What was wrong with her? Knowing that she'd eventually be able to walk out on him had been the one thing
that had sustained her all these ghastly months!

She stood up, suddenly knowing why she was still
holding on to the towel for dear life. Because he *was* her
dear life. Her very dearest. Without him her life was
nothing!

'Fool!' she cried aloud. 'Crass, stupid, naïve, un-
thinking dolt! How could you be so blind?'

All too easy, she saw now. Intent on being her own
person, she had refused to see Randall as he was. But
now that she did, she wanted to grovel at his feet, beg
forgiveness for every wounding word she'd flung at him;
be such a loving, caring wife that he'd——

As swiftly as joy had flooded her, it seeped away,
leaving her bereft. It was hopeless. Randall loved another woman, and their marriage was merely one of
expediency.

'Great!' she muttered. 'The girl who wanted to be
loved for herself is married to a man who wants her only
for her shares!'

Despondently she went into her room. Her hope of a
happy future was so much chaff in the wind, blown away
by the reality of the situation. If she wanted Randall she

would have to be content with being second-best, for, unlike her, when *he* fell in love, it lasted.

But could she bear to remain with him on these terms, or should she walk out the moment she was free to do so? Yet why should she? She wasn't Ed Harris's daughter for nothing! Randall might not be in love with her, but he wasn't immune to her, and though he had been more passionate than loving, it was basis for her to work on.

And let's face it, she thought, sex was an important part of marriage. If a couple weren't physically compatible, then sure as hens laid eggs, the marriage would founder.

OK, she had one plus on her side. Another was propinquity, and from now on where Randall went she would follow, brightening his days, learning about his work so she could discuss it with him intelligently, making Oakland a loving home filled with laughter, friends, family.

Family? Funny, she'd never thought of children in relation to Barry. Yet with Randall it was all too easy, proving how deeply he had entered her heart.

She puzzled over the reason. Was it his strength or the dry humour she had come to appreciate? Or perhaps it was the sharpness of his mind. Even as she acknowledged it was all of these, she knew that most important was his kindness, and the way he had sustained her during her father's critical days.

Restlessly she returned to the bathroom to shower. Should she tell Randall about her change of heart? The very prospect made her squirm. Better to let her behaviour speak for her, and, being Randall, he'd soon realise what she was telling him!

Hot water needled her skin, running in rivulets down the breasts he had tenderly touched, and reminding her of so much more that she trembled and ached for him.

Hurriedly drying herself, she donned the most colourful dress she had brought with her. If only there was no other woman in his life! She sighed, wondering how to get the better of a rival she had never met. Oh God! Every time a female came into their orbit she'd wonder if it was the one. Randall had said she had the same colouring as herself, and although it wasn't the greatest thing to go on, tawny blondes weren't all that run of the mill. She'd keep her eyes open—and her ears too in case he gave anything else away. Strangely enough she wasn't afraid he would cheat on her, and this filled her with another upsurge of love. He was streets above any other man she had met.

The telephone rang again and her joy turned to disappointment as she heard Barry's voice.

'Hi!' he said breezily. 'Just checking if you were safely tucked up before your husband got home last night.'

'Of course.' She saw herself framed in the mirror opposite—a tall, slender girl with long, flyaway hair and honey-gold eyes, their innocence contradicting the lie she was politely uttering.

'Are you free to lunch with me today?' he went on.

'We're leaving for Norfolk this afternoon.'

'I can meet you twelve-thirty at our usual place?'

'The answer's still no.'

'Make it yes,' he urged. 'When I think how I behaved last night I could cut my throat, and if you'd let me grovel in person...'

'It isn't necessary.'

'*Please*, Sandra.'

She stifled a chuckle, thinking his speech could equally well be said by Randall, and the knowledge prompted her to be magnanimous.

'Very well, the Ritz at twelve-thirty.'

It wasn't until she was on her way there that she questioned the wisdom of her decision. If Randall were to find out ... But she would take care he didn't, and after today she would cut Barry from her life.

Sitting opposite him in the crowded restaurant, she marvelled she had ever been taken in by him. Comparing him with Randall was like comparing tapwater with spring, the ersatz with the genuine.

'Reminds me of the good old days,' Barry said when they had placed their orders.

'Not quite.'

His slight smile told her he had got the point, which he proved by keeping the conversation to business. 'Do you enjoy being a lady of leisure?' he asked her as they tackled the main course.

'I'm not. I'm helping someone finish a children's book, and then plan to do one of my own.'

She expanded on her idea, but he only half listened, eager to hold the floor with the clever campaigns he was working on, unlike Randall who was a listener and encouraged her to talk.

Bored by Barry's bragging, Sandra was on tenterhooks to get back to Randall and tell him straight out that she had no intention of leaving him and would do her best to make their marriage work. She might even, with a little encouragement, confess she loved him. But that would depend on his reaction to her statement.

'Mind if we skip coffee?' she asked, declining a sweet. 'I'm not sure when Randall's due back and I don't like keeping him waiting.'

'Quite the loving wife!'

'Yes, I am,' she said, silently vowing to be, and hiding her impatience as Barry paid the bill and led her out to his car. The traffic was bad, and it was some twenty minutes later before she had said goodbye to him and was crossing the hotel lobby towards the lift. As she reached it, Randall stepped out. Colour flamed her cheeks as sight of him brought last night back to her, and as if he sensed it, his hand lightly touched her arm and lingered there.

'I finished early,' he said softly, 'and went up to find you. Was your shopping successful?'

Sandra didn't have a single package to show for it, and her colour deepened. 'I—er—I——'

'I believe this is yours, madam.' One of the porters held out a green umbrella to her. 'The young gentleman in the Porsche said you left it behind.'

It was impossible for Sandra to go any redder, and she practically snatched the umbrella from him and went blindly into the lift.

In icy silence Randall followed her, not uttering a word till they were in the seclusion of their suite.

'I thought I'd made it clear I didn't want you seeing your boyfriend.' His very calm signified fury. 'If you'd like another lesson, I'm ready to give you one.'

She was speechless. She knew he had begun making love to her as a punishment, but that he still saw it as such was so demeaning that she lashed out at him.

'Don't threaten me, Randall, or I'll walk out on you right now!'

'And break your father's heart? I think not.'

'It would hurt him far more if he knew about last night!'

It was Randall's turn to colour, and he swung away from her, his action showing she had found the chink in his armour. He didn't care how much he hurt *her*, but he would do anything not to upset her father!

'You see, two can play the same game,' she went on relentlessly, 'so stop thinking you can blackmail me into obeying you. The reasons I gave you for going out with Barry last night were true, and if you don't believe me, that's *your* problem, not mine.'

'There's still a right and a wrong way to behave.'

'And raping me was right?'

Slowly he turned to face her. 'It was the most crass, appalling thing to have done. And when I found that— that you were still a...' He stopped as if he couldn't bring himself to continue, and furiously Sandra did it for him.

'A virgin? Is that what you find so hard to admit?'

'Yes,' he muttered, 'I do. I'm not trying to excuse my behaviour, but every time I referred to Barry as your lover, you didn't deny it.'

'Because your assumption infuriated me. Anyway, it was none of your business!'

'It is now.'

'You mean you'd have controlled your passion if you'd known?' she sneered.

Several seconds passed without his answering, but she didn't attempt to guess his thoughts, for he was too poker-faced. She tried to remain emotionally detached, but was painfully conscious of his height and leanness, of the fine-boned hands hanging loosely at his sides, hands which had aroused her as no others had ever done.

'I can't give you an honest answer,' he said finally, 'because I don't know it. Remaining on good terms with one's ex—be they lover or husband—is par for the course these days, and maybe if circumstances had been normal between us, I wouldn't have reacted as violently.'

With his calm, graceful tread he crossed over to the window and, with his back to the pale spring sun, was but a dark shadow. 'I despise myself for what happened, and if it were possible for us to part here and now... But unfortunately we're stuck with each other for the moment. If you can find it in your heart to forgive me, you have my word I'll never touch you again.'

Sandra perched on the arm of the settee, her body shaking with misery. So much for her high hopes of a happy future! Smarting from the blow he had dealt her, she lashed out,

'I'm amazed your conscience pains you enough to let me go! Won't it jeopardise your position in the company? After all, I'll be the largest shareholder, and I might well try to have you removed.'

'That's a chance I must take. But one thing's certain: our marriage was a mistake, and we'll rectify it as soon as we can.'

Their return journey to Oakland was only made bearable by the presence of Peter Salmon, one of Randall's assistants. Sandra had not known he was coming down with them, and suspected it was a spur-of-the-moment decision on Randall's part to prevent the two of them travelling alone together. Only as they entered the house did she hear that Peter was also staying to dinner, and it made her decide to go to see her father.

'I'd rather you didn't drive round the countryside on your own at night,' Randall murmured.

She was on the point of arguing when she saw Peter watching them intently. 'Then I'll leave it till morning,' she shrugged, turning to the stairs. 'I'll have dinner upstairs anyway. Then the two of you can talk business to your hearts' content!'

Once alone, she called her father for a chat, then slipped into a housecoat, wryly regretting her decision to have dinner in her room, where she was alone with thoughts she didn't want to dwell on. But she had made her choice and must make the best of it, as she must this present situation.

And what an incredible situation it was! A woman who could never have the man she wanted, any more than the man she wanted could have the woman *he* loved.

CHAPTER THIRTEEN

SANDRA threw herself into her work as the best way of keeping her mind off Randall. She still had a few drawings to do for Dominic's story and was eager to get them out of the way so she could concentrate on her own book.

Daily the snow leopard was growing more real to her, not least because she associated it with Randall. Yet by rights she should consign the animal to limbo and find another one to inspire her. Fat chance of that, though, when the leopard and Randall were inextricably interwoven in her heart!

Two weeks' work round the clock saw the Dominic book sent to the publishers, after which she decided to let her mind lie fallow for a few days.

The weekend loomed ahead of her and she debated how to fill it. Aileen was visiting a textile factory in Milan, and Randall—if this week followed the pattern of the other two—would be closeted in his study with Peter or other assistants. He was working flat-out, and she had no means of knowing if it was necessary or deliberate.

Saturday was a glorious spring day and she spent it with her father. Some of the rhododendrons were in bloom, forming a glorious bank of colour by the small lake at the far end of the lawn, and they strolled down to look at them.

'Why didn't Randall come over with you?' Edward Harris grumbled, as they slowly wended their way back to the house.

'He's very busy.'

'Even so, he should take a breather. It's up to you to see he doesn't work himself into the ground.'

'I'll take him to Paris next weekend and Rome the weekend after.' Sandra giggled at her father's expression. 'Well, you did say you wanted him to relax, didn't you?'

'Nearer home, girl. No need to go to extremes!'

Yet going to extremes was what she always did, Sandra admitted to herself as she drove home through the dusk, and she doubted she could ever change. Resolutely she tried to think of her father instead of Randall. But that brought her full circle back to Randall, for she had noticed how frail her father had looked this afternoon, a frailty that put a big question mark above her future, for when she lost him, she would lose Randall too.

Entering Oakland, she was surprised to see the door of the study open, and glimpsed him sitting jacketless at his desk.

'Still at it?' she asked lightly.

'Just finished.' He yawned and stretched his arms above his head.

Her eyes went instantly to his flexing muscles, and a tremor curled like a snake across her stomach.

'I didn't expect you back so soon,' he added, rising and coming towards her.

'Daddy was tired.' She inched away from him. 'We can have dinner early if you like.'

'Good idea.' He paused. 'You've been burning the candle pretty late at night, haven't you?'

'So have you, or you wouldn't have noticed!'

'Still pining for Barry?' he questioned.

'And *you* for your Lady of the Camellias?'

'Such interest in her! If I didn't know you better, I'd think you were jealous!'

With commendable aplomb, Sandra laughed. 'Just staggered that anyone can touch your heart.'

He went to reply, thought better of it, and swung back to his study.

Sandra had her foot on the stair when she heard the telephone ring, and an instant later Randall called to her.

'It's your boyfriend. Want to take it upstairs?'

'Why? I'm sure you'll enjoy hearing me talk to him!' She swaggered past him to the desk and lifted the receiver. Trust Barry to call at the most inopportune moment.

'Barry!' she said, her tone belying her thoughts. 'How lovely to hear from you.'

'Sorry to bother you at the weekend, honey,' he said without preamble, 'but Arnie Jackson insists I get your opinion on the new layouts our art department have done for him.'

'That's crazy!' she exclaimed.

'I won't argue with you there. But you know how highly he rates you, and if it makes him happy to know you approve them...'

'What if I think they're awful?'

'Have a heart, will you! Look, I'm seeing a client in Norfolk tomorrow, so I'll bring them with me. I hope you're free for lunch?'

Convinced the whole thing was a ploy to see her again—he obviously hadn't accepted that their relationship was over—her instinct was to tell him to take a running jump. But because Randall was listening to her every word she feigned enthusiasm and agreed to meet him at Marco's, an Italian restaurant well known for the delicious dishes cooked by its owner-chef.

'I assume you won't make a scene once I'm back?' she said to Randall as her call ended.

'And I assume you'll be discreet,' he countered frigidly.

'As discreet as you.'

'What's that supposed to mean?'

'That I don't believe you're leading the celibate life you pretend.'

The instant she had spoken, Sandra could have kicked herself. She sounded a shrew, and jealous to boot! That Randall thought so too was evident from the smile that lifted a corner of his mouth, giving him a sardonic look that his tortoiseshell spectacles intensified.

'You haven't worn your gold-rimmed ones for ages,' she blurted out.

It took an instant for him to follow her train of thought. 'These suit my mood.'

'Hard and aggressive?'

'On the contrary—back into my shell,' he corrected.

'Your armour plating, you mean!' She ached with love for him, and her only protection was to stop him guessing it. 'I'm not surprised you're unlucky in love. You're about as easy to get close to as a porcupine!'

'If you've quite finished...'

He sat down at his desk, and with a shrug she sauntered out. But once alone she was furious with herself for losing her temper. What good did it do beyond making him dislike her all the more?

That night they dined together in almost total silence, and though the food threatened to choke her, Sandra forced it down. She'd die rather than let Randall see he'd ruined her appetite! Not that *he* was doing great in the eating stakes. Sharp-eyed, she watched him cut his sole into small pieces and push them round his plate.

'Aren't you hungry?' she asked.

'Arguing robs me of my appetite.' Another piece of sole disappeared underneath his spinach, then, thinking better of it, he speared it with his fork and resumed eating. 'Surely it's possible for us to be civil to one another while we have to stay together? Or do you enjoy being rude?'

'Not necessarily. But you bring out the worst of me.'

'You certainly brought out the worst of me,' Randall said abruptly. 'When I think of that night at the Connaught I hate myself.'

'Forget it. It's over.'

'Have *you* forgotten it?'

She longed to tell him she never would; that what had begun in hate had ended—for her—in love. But pride kept her silent, and she managed an indifferent shrug, as if the whole episode now bored her. What an actress I've become, she thought. Put on a brave front and act uncaring. It must surely be easier to pull hen's teeth!

Dinner over, Randall surprised her by saying he was going out, and even more by not telling her where. Still, he had dozens of friends, though on their return from honeymoon she had insisted she didn't want to get caught up in his social swim.

'For the moment I can use our American take-over as an excuse,' he had informed her, 'but sooner or later you'll have to play your role.'

Now there was no need, for they were both marking time till the parting of their ways. Inexplicably she was reminded of the parting of the Red Sea. Except that the Israelites had escaped to freedom, and she would be escaping to what? Certainly not freedom, but a prison of loneliness, of regret for all she had thrown away.

A sound at the door made her look up, and she saw Maria, the Portuguese maid.

'Mrs Royston here to see you,' the girl said in her careful English, and Sandra's face lit up.

'I thought you were in Milan,' she exclaimed as Aileen, elegant in a multicoloured Missoni suit, came in.

'I flew in earlier than expected, and couldn't face being alone. I shouldn't have come without phoning, but——'

'Don't be silly.' Sympathetically, Sandra went towards her, realising there were occasions when the loss of Dominic overwhelmed her friend. 'I'm delighted you dropped in. Randall's out, though, so you'll have to make do with me.'

'Hardly making do!' Aileen expostulated. 'Don't tell me that workaholic's still working?'

'I haven't a clue.'

The red head tilted. 'Have I come in on a quarrel or something?'

'A quarrel or nothing,' Sandra blurted out. 'That's what our marriage is, I'm afraid. Nothing!'

Aileen made no comment and Sandra liked her for it. Most women would have plied her with questions, using her outburst as a reason to probe. But Aileen made herself comfortable in a chair and started talking about her trip, giving Sandra a chance to compose herself.

But try as she would, Sandra found it impossible. Misery robbed her of discretion, and if she didn't confide in someone, she would explode.

'Our marriage is a sham,' she stated flatly. 'It always has been.'

'A sham? I don't follow.'

'Shows what good actors we are.'

Without emotion, almost as if reciting a laundry list, Sandra gave Aileen a censored version of why she and Randall had married, and had the pleasure—if pleasure it could be called—of seeing her friend's total astonishment.

'You mean—you two don't love each other?'

Sandra could not bring herself to actually lie, and let a lift of her shoulders be her answer. 'You were wrong to think he'd stopped loving that other woman,' she went on. 'As far as I know he still carries a torch for her.'

'I can't take it in. You always seemed so happy together.'

Sandra toyed with the idea of confiding her new-found feelings for Randall, then dismissed it. Much as she liked Aileen, the woman was Randall's friend, and it would be unfair to burden her with the truth, then swear her to secrecy. Except that she had already burdened her with a great deal!

'I can't believe *anyone* can be unhappy married to Randall,' Aileen went on. 'If there isn't someone else in your life, why can't you——'

'You need two to make a marriage work,' Sandra cut in, 'and Randall's finally come to the conclusion that ours won't.'

'That doesn't mean you can't put up a fight for him. Or don't you want to?'

Once more Sandra let a shrug speak for her, and they both fell silent, deep in their own thoughts.

Aileen is far more Randall's kind of woman than I could ever be, Sandra flagellated herself, not for the first time, taking in the petite figure, the heart-shaped face aureoled by that lovely flaming hair. OK, so Randall had only seen Aileen as his best friend's widow, but having finally had a taste of marriage, he might not be averse to taking the plunge a second time. And what better than with this highly attractive and sympathetic woman?

'I'd rather Randall doesn't know that you've told me,' Aileen said suddenly. 'He's such a private person, he'd be embarrassed.'

'You're right. I'm sorry I burdened you with it.'

'Oh, my dear, don't be. That's what friends are for: to be there when you need them, to have a sympathetic ear and a closed mouth.'

Sandra pondered on this for most of a sleepless night, and though she trusted Aileen's discretion, she still regretted her outburst.

With no particular enthusiasm she met Barry for lunch next day. It was like meeting a stranger, and even his compliments on her appearance fell on deaf ears. At first they discussed the graphic work he had brought, and studying the slick layouts she marvelled that she had ever considered making advertising her career.

'No chance of your coming back to Causten's?' he questioned.

'None. I've found my niche and I'm staying in it.'

'Kids' books? Wonders never cease!'

The wonder was she'd ever loved him!

'I hear Harris Pharmaceuticals is looking for a new agency,' she heard him say as he poured the last of their wine. 'You know we've pitched for the account?'

She hadn't, but had no intention of saying so.

'We did a sensational presentation,' he continued. 'Come to think of it, I've a few of the layouts in my briefcase.'

'What a coincidence!' How she managed to keep a straight face she didn't know, but Barry was too full of himself to recognise her sarcasm. Showing her the art work for Arnie Jackson had been so much hot air. All he had wanted was to discuss the Harris Pharmaceutical account, hoping that if *she* liked Causten's ideas it would give them the edge over rival agencies! 'There's no point my looking at the layouts,' she went on casually. 'I never interfere in company affairs.'

'Maybe not,' Barry said, then went on to confirm her suspicions. 'But having worked for us, you could put in a good word on our behalf.'

'It might have the opposite effect. Don't forget Randall knows you were my boyfriend...'

Her words fell upon Barry like a brick on thin ice, shattering his equanimity and doing her a power of good.

'I can't believe your husband would hold that against me,' he muttered. 'Since your marriage we've only been friends.'

Friends? Sandra nearly threw up. She couldn't get away from him fast enough. If Randall had at least told her Causten's was one of the agencies bidding for the company account, she would have known why Barry had wanted to see her. But that was why Randall had kept quiet. He had wanted her humiliated!

As she rounded the driveway of Oakland, tears blurred her vision, and she did not see Randall's car outside the front door until she had drawn up beside it. He was home early! Heart racing, she rushed into the house.

'Sandra, my dear.' The unusual endearment as he came towards her gave her the news she had been dreading, and with a little moan she put her face in her hands, swamped by a desolation too deep for the solace of tears.

'It was very quick,' he said softly. 'He was having a cup of tea, and the next moment was gone.'

Knowing her father hadn't suffered was a comfort Sandra clung to in the sad days that followed, though nothing could mitigate the fact that the one man she had trusted above all others was gone for ever. Added to her filial grief was the realisation that there was nothing to keep her and Randall together any more, and the pain of this soon became apparent in the waxy pallor of her skin, and the fragile bones showing in her slender body.

'It's such a lonely feeling being an orphan,' she said to Randall ten days after her father's death.

'Hardly lonely, with two aunts and uncles and dozens of cousins,' he said calmly, setting down the book he was reading.

'None of them can take the place of a parent.'

'Obviously not. But you're beautiful, wealthy, talented, and have your whole life ahead of you.'

What a lovely picture he's painting for me, she thought. Trouble was he hadn't put himself in it, and consequently it was a picture in black and grey. She braced herself for what was to come, and wasn't one whit surprised when it did.

'You're free to live your own life now,' Randall continued. 'There's nothing to keep you here.'

Only you, Sandra thought miserably, imagining his astonishment if she asked him to let her stay with him, pleaded for his love and said she wanted a real marriage. But she said none of it, and, boarding school influence to the fore, murmured politely, 'I don't fancy living at Wideacres. In fact, I'm putting it on the market. So if I could remain here until I find somewhere...'

'By all means.' His eyes were intent on her. 'Do you plan on remaining in the district?'

Knowing how bitter-sweet this would be, and more bitter than sweet if and when he eventually remarried, she shook her head. 'I'm going to London.'

'Of course. Stupid of me.'

'You're never stupid, Randall.'

'I wish I could endorse that.' His voice was low with a sadness he did not bother hiding. 'I should never have forced you to marry me. At least *you* had the sense to know it was a mistake the day after we got engaged!'

'It's all water under the bridge,' she shrugged. 'I'm not bitter.'

'I'm glad.' He ran a hand over his hair. Though not a worried gesture, it didn't show ease. 'May I take it you've forgiven me for—for what happened at the Connaught?'

Sandra hesitated. If he hadn't made love to her, would she have realised her feelings for him? Eventually yes, though they might have taken longer to surface. But his brutal awakening of her sexuality had catapulted her into a womanhood she only wanted to share with him.

Once again she battled with the urge to fling herself into his arms, and winning it, managed to give a polite 'shall-I-pour-the-tea' smile, as she said, 'That's water under the bridge too, Randall. Let's not paddle in it.'

'How calm you sound!'

'It's one good thing I've learned from you.'

'At the risk of being told to mind my own business, may I remind you that now, more than ever, you're likely to attract fortune-hunters?'

Didn't he think anyone could love her for herself? It was a bleak realisation and a recurring theme in her life.

'Don't worry about me, Randall. If I could see through *you*, I could see through anyone!'

'The cutting tongue has returned, I see, which is my cue to leave.' He went to the door. 'I'll do my best to keep out of your way while you're here. I'd like us to part friends. It's more civilised.'

Would he think it civilised if she flung a teacup at him, if she shouted at him like a fishwife, and she said she'd never let him go?

'Oh, by all means let's be civilised,' she said sweetly. 'I'll even dance at your wedding next time around!'

CHAPTER FOURTEEN

SANDRA stepped back from the easel. Satisfied with what she saw, she dropped her palette on the table, put her brushes in a jar and wandered over to the window. The airy penthouse she had bought gave her a magnificent view of Regent's Park, where now, in mid-autumn, the green leaves were turning to russet. But the gardens at Oakland would still be a mass of flowers: luxuriant roses, thick-headed chrysanthemums, the vivid splash of dahlias.

But Oakland meant Randall, and Randall meant heartache, and she tried to push them both from her mind. Easier to count the hairs on her head! Accepting this, she wallowed in the memory of him as she had last seen him, framed in the doorway of his home the morning she had left him for ever, her cases packed, lipstick bright as her red Mercedes, manner as relaxed as his.

'Don't hesitate to call if you need me,' he had said.

'Thanks,' she had answered, knowing she would rather die than avail herself of the offer, for the only way to forget him was not to see him.

Unfortunately out of sight didn't mean out of mind, and in the months that followed she had longed a thousand times to pick up the telephone and call him on some pretext, just to hear his voice. There were so many reasons she could have given, her huge block of shares in the company being one. But she had resisted, and gradually by throwing herself into work and an active social life she had almost become her own woman. Her own woman. What irony, when she only longed to be his!

She turned from the window, and as she did saw the setting sun reflected in a crystal vase on a table. The shimmering glass reminded her of the wine glass Randall had been holding when she had glimpsed him six weeks ago dining at the St James's Club. She had gone there with Jon Harley—brother of an old school friend—who had unexpectedly re-entered her life when her agent had sent the first chapter of her snow leopard story, together with three illustrations, to a television film director who had declared they would make an excellent children's series if she could devise additional plots.

She had proved her ability by dashing off half a dozen outlines, whereupon he had telephoned to introduce himself.

'You wouldn't be Emma Harley's frog-loving brother?' she had asked, his drawling voice twanging a memory chord.

'You wouldn't be Emma's skinny blonde friend who spent a summer with us in Sardinia?'

Mutual laughter had resulted in dinner together and a blossoming relationship, though the blossoming was more on Jon's side than hers. But as the weeks rolled into months and Randall did not contact her she started seeing Jon more frequently, and the first time he had taken her to the St James's Club she had spied the silver-blond head across the discreetly lit room!

Randall! Looking the same as ever, which meant aloof and patrician, and sitting with someone Sandra had always known in her heart of hearts was the only woman capable of melting the barrier he had erected around himself.

Watching Aileen sparkle up at him as they toasted each other, Sandra realised why the woman had steered clear of her all these weeks. Not that Aileen had made it obvious. She had come to see Sandra's apartment, lunched with her a month later, and telephoned to rejoice with her over the reviews given to Dominic's book.

But for two months there had been no word, not a chirp, not a peep, and the reason was all too evident.

Sipping her drink, Sandra saw Aileen touch her glass to Randall's, and jealousy, swift as a summer storm, drenched her, washing away her belief that she could find happiness with another man. It was Randall or no one, and since it couldn't be Randall, she must make do with a career. She berated herself for letting a single night of love numb her to anyone else's touch. Yet only one pair of hands could bring her tinglingly alive, one mouth arouse her, one pair of loins encompass her.

She shivered, and Jon had eyed her.

'Air-conditioning too cold?'

'No. Just a goose walking over my grave.'

'That would make a good follow-up for your TV series.'

'Graves?'

'No, a goose!' Blue eyes twinkled, and he had raked back a strand of chestnut brown hair. 'They're incredible creatures, you know. Intelligent, funny, ideal subjects for puppetry or animation. Dream up an idea and I'll see if I can get backing for it.'

'Maybe I'll use my own money.'

'No, you won't. If your ideas are commercial, *other* people will finance it. Stop thinking like mega-rich Sandra Harris!'

'That's what I like about you,' she had laughed. 'You watch over my finances as lovingly as my lawyers!'

'I must be trying to prove something,' had come his soft response, 'and I think you know what.'

'I'm still married, Jon,' she reminded him.

'You're going to get divorced, aren't you?'

'Yes. But until I am I'd rather not discuss the future.'

'May we at least drink to the present?'

'Of course.'

It was midnight when they had left the Club. There was no sign of Randall and Aileen, who must have gone while she had been absorbed with Jon, which at least showed she could put Randall to the back of her mind if she tried hard enough.

Trouble was, he kept surfacing, and she found the only way to keep him submerged was by concentrating on the snow leopard and the other characters with whom she surrounded him.

After a particularly gruelling session which left her with a dull but persistent headache, she took herself for a brisk walk through Regent's Park where children were feeding the geese and ducks, old people chatted on the park benches, and a few young lovers strolled hand in hand.

Despondency washed over her, and on an impulse she left the Park and hailed a cab to take her to her favourite boutique in Bond Street. It was hard to be extravagant when you had the money to buy what you liked, but she did her level best, and emerged laden with parcels at the very moment that Aileen stepped out of the next-door gallery.

For the briefest instant the woman seemed disconcerted, then gave a wide smile.

She looks ten years younger, Sandra noted with a pang, and swallowed the question uppermost in her mind, knowing that to utter it would be a giveaway.

'Lovely to see you,' they both murmured, giving each other the cheek-to-cheek kiss in the air of modern-day woman, and reverting to a silence unusual for them.

'I've been meaning to call you,' Aileen broke it, 'but I wasn't sure you wanted to see me.'

'That should be my line,' Sandra responded.

'Why?'

'Well, you were Randall's friend first.'

'But you aren't his enemy,' countered Aileen, then went on candidly, 'I rather felt you wanted to forget everyone associated with him.'

'But not you,' Sandra said quickly. 'If it weren't for you pushing me into finishing the illustrations for Dominic's book, I wouldn't have dreamed of doing a children's one of my own.'

'Ah, yes,' Aileen beamed. 'I read somewhere that your snow leopard's being made into a children's series. You must be over the moon.'

'I am,' Sandra confessed, but didn't add that it was the only thing that made her days bearable. 'What about you? Busy with a new textile collection?'

'In the plural. A silk one for a Japanese firm and a wool one for the Italians.' Aileen linked her arm through Sandra's. 'It's so good talking to you again. We really mustn't let our friendship lapse. And if you don't want me to mention Randall, I won't.'

Fat lot of good that will do, mused Sandra. Just being with Aileen brought him close.

'Do you see much of him?' she asked casually.

'When I can tear him away from his work.' Aileen blinked rapidly, as if embarrassed, and Sandra, fed up with discretion, said boldly, 'You'd be silly to let him get away.'

'A few weeks ago I'd have agreed with you, but now I'm not so sure. He'd bring Dominic back for me, and a threesome in a marriage won't work.'

This wasn't what Aileen had said in New York, and Sandra wondered if she meant it or was being discreet. Either way it didn't matter. Randall could do as he liked with his life.

They parted with the mutual promise to keep in touch, and Sandra returned home. Once there, she hung away the clothes she had bought without bothering to look at them, slipped into a smock and perched on the stool at her drawing table which she kept permanently set up in one corner of her living-room.

She studied three of her most recent illustrations for her story. How alive the leopard seemed, his fur so rich and glossy she almost felt its texture beneath her fingertips. Half smiling, she relived the plot she had created around him: her poor, short-sighted leopard growing thinner by the day because he couldn't see well enough to hunt, until a tender-hearted doe—finding a pair of spectacles in the back of a hunter's jeep—had conquered her fear of the leopard long enough to place them in his path.

The instant he put them on, the leopard's courage returned—though not his desire to kill, for his days of blindness had made him 'see' that the animals he had once enjoyed hunting were the same creatures who had taken pity on him and fed him tit-bits to keep him alive. And so the snow leopard, who had begun by being coldly ferocious, had his vulnerability shown to him and had grown warm and loving in the process.

Staring at the last drawing, Sandra remembered how Randall's vulnerability had been revealed to her on learning of his continuing love for a woman who hadn't wanted him. But unlike the leopard, new glasses wouldn't help him see the situation differently!

The doorbell brought her to her feet, and peeping through the spy hole, she saw Jon.

'I was passing and took a chance you'd be home,' he said as he came in. 'If I'm interrupting——'

'You are, but I'm glad.'

In tan slacks and bronze shirt, he was very much a macho man. If she could love to order, she would be head over heels about him; as it was, she felt only affection.

'Fancy a Pimms?' she asked.

'Sounds great.'

Filling two glasses, she set them on a table on the terrace, where Jon was already lounging in a hammock.

'Picture of a busy man,' she grinned.

'And enjoying every minute,' he grinned back. 'What's nicer than an afternoon lolling in the sunshine with a luscious lovely? All we need is a lapping sea and soft music.'

'No problem supplying the music.' She pressed a switch let into the wall, and the air was instantly filled with a Beethoven concerto.

'Anything lighter?' asked Jon.

She flipped another switch, and hearing the news, was about to press again when the words 'Harris Pharmaceuticals' left her hand in mid-air. Increasing the volume, she heard with mounting horror that an explosion had ripped apart one of the laboratories. Two people were dead, six had been rescued and six were still unaccounted for, including the Managing Director, Randall Pearson, who had been first on the scene after the explosion, and had been helping evacuate staff when a second explosion had torn through the building.

For a split second Sandra sat paralysed, then she jumped to her feet, glass crashing to the floor.

'Randall! I must go to him.' She ran into the room for her car keys, and was at the front door when Jon's hand stopped her.

'You're in no state to drive. I'll take you.'

'It's not necessary. I'll be fine.'

'But——'

'*Please!* I'd rather drive myself.'

'Get going, then. I'll lock up here and leave the keys with the porter.' He caught her shoulder in a warm grip. 'Think positive, darling.'

'He may be dead!'

'Or alive.' He gave her a shake. 'If he is, tell him you love him. You do, don't you?'

She nodded, pulled free, and ran to the elevator.

As she speeded out of London, she remembered how often she had rushed back to Norfolk in a panic. First to get away from Barry, then to see her father, and now because Randall was in danger—might even be dead!

Of all her journeys this was the worst. While Randall was alive, she could still cling to the hope that one day he might be hers. But if he were dead, her life would simply be years to be endured. It was a terrifying thought and she made a conscious effort to calm herself. But as she drew nearer to the plant, her agitation increased. Please God, don't let him be dead! I'll do anything, only please let him be alive!

Breasting a rise, she saw a plume of dark smoke in the sky ahead. Heart pounding, she pressed harder on the accelerator, hands tight on the wheel, tears blurring her eyes. The main gates came in sight. Police stood guard at them, holding back photographers and newsmen wanting to get closer to the smoking building that could be glimpsed behind the main factory. Polluted air filled her nostrils as she lowered the window and handed her driver's licence to a policeman. He glanced at it, then let her through.

Parking in the forecourt of the office block, she headed for the laboratory, taking a policeman's advice and wrapping a scarf yashmak fashion round her face. Several fire engines were slowly moving away, but ambulances were arriving to join those already there, and a large tent, with doctors and nurses milling about, was set up to one side.

Desperately Sandra buttonholed a young woman with a stethoscope. 'Has everyone been rescued? Is there any news of Randall Pearson—a tall, blond man?'

''Fraid I don't know—I only got here a few moments ago. But I heard the firemen have doused the fire and are donning gas-masks to go in.'

Gas-masks! It was becoming more horrific by the minute. Sandra pushed her way through the throng to get closer to the laboratory.

'Best not go nearer,' a fireman warned as he staggered past, eyes red and streaming, face blackened with smoke.

'I'm looking for my husband!' she cried.

'Relatives are waiting over there.' He pointed to a group of people huddling close together as if for comfort.

But Sandra had no intention of joining them and, swinging round, was about to rush back to the tent when a loud cheer made her turn to see the waiting crowd surge forward as firemen emerged from the laboratory supporting smoke-blackened figures.

'There's my son!' a woman cried excitedly.

Her voice spurred the crowd on, and police linked arms to stop them, allowing only ambulancemen to get through.

Accepting that she would never get past them, Sandra darted from one ambulance to the other to check who had been rescued. None was Randall and, sobbing with fear, she hurried into the tent.

It was teeming with the injured, some on stretchers, some on chairs, but Randall wasn't here either. Numbly she refused to look at the dark-windowed black vehicle parked on the far side of the tent. Yet it loomed large in her mind's eye and she gasped with the pain of it, the sound dying in her throat as silvery fair hair streaked with black came into her line of vision. It wasn't... It was Randall!

Her limbs went weak with relief, her world righted itself, and she sent up a silent prayer of thanks, her eyes never leaving the dishevelled figure pausing wearily—almost as if in slow motion—to remove his glasses and search in his pocket for a handkerchief to clean them. As he pulled it out, a shower of dust came with it, and Sandra rushed forward and took the glasses from him.

'Let me do that,' she said tremulously.

At the sound of her voice, Randall looked up. 'Sandra! What are *you* doing here?'

'I heard about the explosion on the news and I came straight down. I thought you were—I wasn't sure if...' Her face crumpled and she started crying. 'I thought you were dead!'

'Only the good die young,' he said whimsically, touching the hand holding his glasses. 'You offered to clean them for me.'

Hurriedly she began, fumbling so nervously at the task that he took them from her, rubbing a finger over the lenses and put them on.

'Go back to the house,' he said softly. 'Breathing in these fumes won't do you any good.'

'What about you?'

'I'm needed here.'

'Then I'll stay till you're ready to go.'

'That might be hours.'

She didn't deign to answer, and, giving her an odd look, Randall strode towards the tent.

Sandra lost count of the hours as she helped tend the injured. The serious burn cases were flown by helicopter to the nearest burns unit, while those with other injuries were taken to hospital in Norwich. Slowly the tent emptied, and she was clearing away a pile of blood-stained clothes when Randall joined her.

'Let's go home,' he said quietly. 'You look all in.'

So did he, she thought, following him to his car. A driver was at the wheel and they climbed into the back seat. Only as she sank into the soft leather did the trauma of the last few hours hit her, and she started trembling.

Randall took her hand. 'You should have gone to Oakland when I suggested it. There was no need for you to stay.'

'There was every need! I'm just—just hungry. I'll feel better when I've eaten.'

'And had a bath,' he added. 'We both stink to high heaven!'

Sandra managed a little laugh, then lapsed into silence as the lights of the house came in view. She experienced a sense of homecoming as she and Randall entered the hall and were greeting by the housekeeper and her husband and a tearful Maria. Randall was clearly touched by their concern for him, and after assuring them he was unhurt, he put a hand under Sandra's elbow and led her upstairs.

A sudden attack of nerves overcame her as they reached the landing, and it was an effort to hide it, though she managed to say calmly, 'What room do I use?'

'The one you've always used.'

'But it was originally yours. Haven't you moved back to it?'

'Yes—but I felt you'd be happier in familiar surroundings.'

Surprised by his concern, she went into the bedroom she had taken over from him when she had come here as his bride. The pastel sheets she had favoured had been replaced by brown ones, and the bowls of flowers on the dressing-table and beside the recamier had given way to rare, bound books. A maroon silk dressing-gown lay across the bed and suede slippers stood neatly on the floor. A small onyx clock ticked merrily away on the bedside table, partially obscuring a silver-framed photograph.

Sandra's heart leapt into her throat. Was she about to see what Randall's lady love looked like? Glancing behind her to make sure he had gone, she hurried across to it, stopping dead at her first clear sight of the picture. It was of her! With shaking fingers she picked it up, and looking at her smiling face, remembered Randall had snapped it on one of the rare occasions he had been free to be with her during their trip to New York. They had gone to Central Park to feed the squirrels and, amused by their antics, she had laughed and offered *him* a handful of nuts! And here was that very moment, framed in silver and on his bedside table.

But why?

Many answers came to mind but none seemed feasible and, still mystified, she went into the bathroom to wash her hair and shower. For the first time in hours she felt clean and fragrant, except for having to put on her acrid-smelling clothes! She was debating whether she dared go down to dinner in a bathrobe when there was a knock at the door and Maria walked in.

'Mr Pearson he ask me to say you left clothes here,' she said. 'They in the blue guest room.'

Wrapping her bathrobe tightly around her, Sandra padded sown the corridor. Only when she saw the number of dresses in the wardrobe did she realise what an emotional state she must have been in when she had left Randall, for here were half the clothes she had bought in New York! They were all too glamorous for a simple evening at home, but since she had no choice... Ruefully she chose a short dress in so fine a wool that it could have been woven by a spider. The soft pink warmed skin still pale from shock and she rummaged in her purse for make-up. All she had was lipstick of the wrong colour and she had to content herself with brushing her hair and catching it away from her face with two grips. She grimaced at them, then pulled them out and let her hair hand loose to her shoulders. She looked like a schoolgirl, but who cared?

Randall was in the conservatory when she came downstairs, brown slacks and matching shirt emphasising his fairness. With the grime removed she saw the dark bruise running down his face and, aware of her eyes   on it, he gave a faint smile.

'It looks worse than it is.'

'How did you get it?'

'A Bunsen burner fell on me.'

'Don't joke,' she said crossly. 'You could have been killed today!'

'I could have been a lot of things,' he said enigmatically, and moved to the dining-room.

'I don't think I can eat this late,' she murmured.

'It's only a snack.'

'A pretty sumptuous one,' she commented amusedly as she saw the assortment of cheeses, pâté and breads. It was the crisp rolls that revived her appetite, and she lavishly buttered one and spread it with *foie gras*.

Randall only picked at his food. Little wonder he had lost weight, Sandra thought, if this was the way he ate.

'For someone who wasn't hungry, you didn't do too badly,' he teased as they returned to the drawing-room.

'I always eat when I'm nervous,' she said, regretting her reply when she saw his eyebrows rise.

'You're not scared of *me*, surely?'

'Well, we hardly parted friends, and it wasn't easy coming back.'

'But you did.'

'Because I thought you might be dead and——'

'But I'm not,' he cut in, 'and though you mightn't think we're friends, I hope you don't consider us enemies?'

'Oh no, never that.'

'Good. I'll always be your friend, you know.'

'Will you?'

'How can you doubt it? A friend is someone who wishes you well, and I'll always wish you that.'

She wondered what he would say if she told him she wanted his love, not his friendship. But pride held her in its grip, and instead she muttered that it was late and she must be leaving for London.

'You look too tired to drive,' he argued. 'Stay over and go back in the morning.'

Sandra nodded, happy that she would be seeing him again tomorrow. What a laugh he'd have if he knew!

'How badly was the laboratory damaged?' she asked, grasping at the first thing that came into her mind.

'It's completely gutted. But luckily the new lab wasn't touched.'

'Do they know what caused the explosion?'

'Not yet.' He lapsed into silence and the minutes ticked by. 'Why didn't you acknowledge me that night at the St James's Club?' he asked abruptly.

She raised her eyes to his. 'You—you saw me?'

'I'm not blind, and you're a very noticeable young woman.'

'You were with Aileen,' she defended. 'I didn't want to intrude.' She forced a smile to her lips. 'You should marry her, Randall. She'll make you an excellent wife.'

'You said that to me before. And to set the record straight, I've no intention of marrying again.'

'Why do——' she stopped. On the verge of mentioning her photograph, embarrassment choked off the words.

'You were saying?' he questioned.

'It was nothing.'

'Then why so edgy?'

She did not answer, and he spoke again.

'You weren't with Barry at the Club that night.'

The abrupt transition of subject caught her off guard. 'I—er—haven't seen him for ages.'

'You mean it's over between you?'

'It was never on—you read more into it than there was,' she told him.

'But you were in love with him.'

'I imagined I was. But a few months away from him made me come to my senses.'

'So who's the new man in your life?' Randall's voice was toneless. 'The one whose eyes you were smiling into?'

Sandra had been totally unaware of doing so, and was intrigued that Randall had thought she had.

'He's producing the film series of my snow leopard,' she explained. 'He's already pre-sold them in the States.'

'That's terrific! I always knew you'd be a success.'

'Have you ever been wrong about anything, Randall?' she asked wryly.

'Sometimes.'

'For example?'

'Do you enjoy digging into wounds?' he demanded with unexpected savagery. 'Why did you have to come down here, anyway? Couldn't you have just called to check if I was alive or dead?'

Shaken by this unexpected attack on her, Sandra rose to walk out, but found her legs wouldn't carry her.

'I'm sorry,' he said jerkily. 'It—it's been a hell of a day and I... Forgive me.'

She acknowledged the apology with a slight movement of her head. 'Will you initiate the divorce or shall I?'

'You've no grounds.'

She swallowed hard. 'Shall I—do you want me to give *you* grounds?'

'You mean there *are* some?'

It took a second for his implication to penetrate, then her face flooded with colour and her first instinct was to say 'Yes, yes, I've been to bed with Jon and every other man I've gone out with!' But hardly had the notion entered her head than she discarded it, knowing she had already told Randall too many lies, and determined not tell him any more.

'I'll discuss it with my lawyer and see what he suggests,' she said, speaking slowly to control the tremor in her voice. 'If you—you'd rather I went back to London tonight, I can do so.'

'There's no need.'

The words were right, but his tone made it plain he didn't wish for her company and she opened the door. 'I'll ask Maria to make up one of the guest rooms for me. In case I don't see you in the morning, perhaps you'll—perhaps you'll telephone to let me know how the injured technicians are doing?'

'I'll see you're kept in the picture.'

'Thank you.'

They were talking like strangers and it struck at her heart, the more so as she knew she had no one to blame except herself. If she hadn't behaved so stupidly when they had become engaged, they might have had an entirely different relationship now.

Lying in the wide double bed in the guest-room furthest from Randall's suite, Sandra flagellated herself with all the might-have-beens, her thoughts lingering longest on the few short months of her marriage. Yet short though they were, they had matured her into a woman, one who would love Randall for the rest of her life and would mourn her inability to make him live her in return.

Restlessly she twisted and turned, nude between the sheets—an unaccustomed freedom which, though enjoyable, added to the strangeness of her already strange position here as unloved wife in her husband's home. She sighed heavily. Randall had married her to safeguard his position in the company, yet had sent her packing as soon as her father died, showing her quite clearly that he preferred taking his chances with the company rather than have his conscience go on pricking him. At least if she was out of his life, he could forget how nearly he had raped her. But then why did he have her photograph beside his bed?

It didn't make sense.

Sitting up, she switched on the lamp, hoping the light would dispel the demons gnawing at her like rats in a corn vat. Why did Randall want to see her face last thing at night and first thing in the morning? No amount of puzzling over the question provided her with the answer, and she knew that unless she had it, it would haunt her for ever. Besides, she couldn't bear him to go on thinking her a flighty, uncaring young woman incapable of deep emotion. She had to put the record straight on *that* at least, even if it led him to guess she loved him.

Without pausing to think, she jumped out of bed, flung on the terry towelling robe and hurried down the corridor to his suite. The lobby was in darkness, but a sliver of light under the bedroom door showed he was not yet asleep. Drawing a deep breath, she knocked, and at his call went in. He was in bed reading, the pink glow of a lamp lighting up the large bruise down the side of his face.

'What's wrong?' he asked sharply.

Now that she was facing him she bitterly regretted her precipitate action in coming here, in being willing to lose face and him see what he meant to her. It would do nothing more than give him a good laugh and make an amusing anecdote for Aileen or any other woman he married. Except that he said he had no intention of marrying anyone. Not that she believed him. He was too virile to be happy without a woman, and he wasn't the type for casual affairs. He'd probably have a longstanding liaison with Aileen—which would inevitably lead to permanence.

'Well?' he cut across her thoughts, 'what do you want?'

'It's about my photograph.' Mortified, Sandra heard the words escape her, and had no choice but to go on. 'If you can't bear having me here for the night, how come you keep my photograph on your bedside table?' She took a step forward, a strange sense of triumph coursing through her as she saw Randall glance quickly at   the
silver-framed picture barely a foot from him.

'Why do you think?' he said tonelessly.

'I haven't a clue.'

'You never have where I'm concerned,' came his bitter reply. 'Why does *anyone* keep a photograph of someone beside their bed?'

'It can't be because you love me! The minute my father died you told me I was free to go.'

'What did you expect me to say when I knew you couldn't wait to leave?' He ran a hand through his hair in an uncharacteristic gesture of impatience. 'Look, this conversation's serving no purpose, and I suggest you return to your room.'

'I only came here because I was curious,' she confessed.

'It killed the cat, you know!' The dry humour was back, turning him into the Randall she knew. 'Curious as to my dastardly reasons for wanting to marry you, curious about the woman I've loved for years, and now about this photograph.'

'Is that surprising?' she came back at him. 'You enjoy making a mystery of things.'

'Regard it as a form of self-preservation. Opening yourself to another person can make you vulnerable.'

'Then remain behind your wall!' she retorted. 'I couldn't care less.'

She was almost at the door when his voice stopped her. 'If I answer one question for you, Sandra, it will help all the others fall into place.'

Intrigued, she glanced round at him, and their eyes met.

'It was *you*,' he said softly. '*You* were my Lady of the Camellias.'

'*Me*?' She couldn't credit what she was hearing. 'But Aileen said——'

'The truth. That for years I'd loved a woman who didn't love *me*.'

'And *I'm* the one? But why didn't you tell me?'

'I did—on your eighteenth birthday—but you wouldn't believe me. You never have. You preferred to think I wanted you because it would safeguard my position in the company.'

'You didn't try very hard to disabuse my mind,' she muttered.

'I'd never have succeeded. You enjoyed thinking the worst of me.'

'That's true.' She was shamefaced and could not pretend otherwise. 'I still think it would have helped if you'd been honest with me.'

'I thought it best to wait until we'd been married a while. I rather hoped you'd see for yourself how I felt about you. Then of course I ruined it all by forcing you to—to...'

The silence lengthened, and when next he spoke, he was prosaic. 'To set the record straight, I have as many shares in the company as you, Sandra, and I also have the authority to act for another large shareholder. So you see, if it came to a straight fight between us I'd win.'

'Then you never had any need to marry me?' she questioned incredulously and, overwhelmed by love, ran towards him. Her towelling robe dragged across the carpet and she stumbled, the wrap parting momentarily to show she had nothing on underneath.

'Do you mind if we finish this discussion tomorrow?' Randall asked in a strangulated voice. 'I'm not made of steel, you know.'

'Nor am I. I'm a flesh and blood woman and I want you!'

'If this is some game——'

'It's for real!' she cried, kneeling on the floor beside his bed and staring up into his face. 'I love you, Randall. I love you so much that when I thought you were injured, perhaps dead, I didn't want to go on living! That's when I decided that if you were spared I'd tell you the truth, but you were so cool and offhand, I thought you didn't want me.'

'Don't you know you're the only person I want?' he said in an agonised tone. 'That without you I really am the zombie you once called me?'

'Don't!' she cried. 'Don't remind me of all the horrible things I said to you!'

With gentle hands he drew her up from the floor on to the bed, but he didn't try to take her in his arms, and she had the impression he was still unsure of her.

'I do love you, Randall,' she reiterated. 'And you might as well know I realised it that night at the Connaught!'

It was as if a lamp had been lit within him: his skin glowed, his eyes sparkled, and the years seemed to fall away from him.

'You mean it?' he breathed.

'With all my heart.'

She had no chance to say more, for he bent and pressed his mouth to hers, his hands fumbling at her fleecy robe till it fell away, leaving her alabaster skin bare to his touch.

'Are you really here,' he whispered against her throat, 'in my room, in my arms?'

'In your bed, too,' she teased and, suiting her actions to her words, slipped between the sheets to press herself close to him.

His response was instantaneous—muscles flexing, limbs tightening, stirring manhood evident.

'We've both been such fools,' Sandra murmured against his chest. 'We're lucky to be given a second chance.'

'I know.' His hands stroked her. 'If it hadn't been for the explosion...'

She pulled slightly away from him to look into his face. 'Would you have divorced me without telling me how you felt?'

'I'm not sure. After you moved out I did my best to forget you, but soon realised I never would. I'd planned on coming to see you when you walked into the St James's Club, but you were so radiant I was convinced you didn't give a damn about me.'

'I thought exactly the same when I saw *you* with Aileen! Oh, Randall, how close we came to parting for ever!'

'Don't remind me.'

His fingers lightly brushed the smooth line of her throat before moving down to rub the rose-red nipples. They hardened at his touch, sending a shiver of desire arcing through her, and she fell back against the pillows and pulled him on top of her, delighting in the tremors of passion that racked him, and marvelling at his self-control in not entering her.

'I want you,' she breathed upon his mouth.

'I'll never let you go again,' he warned. 'No other man will ever be your lover.'

'You're my one and only,' she smiled at him, but he did not smile back. 'What's wrong, Randall?'

'I'm the one with curiosity now,' he admitted. 'Why was I the first, Sandra? You're so beautiful I can't believe no other man tried to make love to you.'

'I never let anyone get to first base,' she said in a small voice. 'Even with Barry I couldn't. That's why we quarrelled. But with *you* it was different.' She paused, then went on, 'Though I fought you in the beginning, I soon found I didn't want to. That's when I realised you'd chased away my demon.' She paused again, drew a deep breath and said in a rush, 'A demon called Mario. He tried to—he made——'

'Darling, don't,' Randall cut in. 'I don't need to know.'

'But I want to tell you. I don't want any secrets between us.'

In a voice that was often so low it was barely audible, she told him of the holiday she had spent with her father in Venice, where they had stayed with friends of his and she had fallen head over heels in love with Mario, the young son of the household.

For the first week the young Italian had been an ideal escort. Then the ingenuous puppy love of a fifteen-year-old girl had gone to his head, and one night he had come to her room where, refusing to take her vehement 'No!' for an answer, he had roughly begun molesting her. For what had seemed an aeon she had fought him silently, ashamed to raise the household lest they believe she had egged him on. But finally fear of him superseded all other considerations, and she had begun screaming. Her cries had brought the household running, and though Mario had tried to bluff it out by insisting Sandra had encouraged him, her father had soon shaken the truth out of him.

It had been an ugly scene, and one which had inevitably destroyed her father's friendship with Mario's parents. For a long while afterwards Sandra had blamed herself for this and wondered whether, in her innocence, she had indeed given Mario the wrong impression of herself.

'You were blameless,' Randall assured her now. 'Mario was as big a swine to you as I was.'

Startled that Randall should equate himself with the Italian, Sandra went to protest, but was stopped by his fingers on her mouth.

'No, darling,' he said soberly, 'my behaviour was no better than Mario's.'

'That's not quite true,' she insisted. 'Anyway, I soon realised the emotions you aroused in me were far different from any I'd ever experienced. If I'd continued fighting you, you wouldn't have gone on. But I encouraged you because I wanted you to love me, though I was too shy to put it into words.

Randall sighed heavily. 'If I could honestly believe you, I wouldn't hate myself so much.'

'Forget hate,' she urged. 'Think only of love.' Delicately she licked his lips with the tip of her tongue. 'When are we going to start that family you always talked about?'

'Not for a long while.' His voice was deep with passion as he responded to her touch. 'I want to know your body first, to love you and love you and love you with no holds barred!'

'What a delicious prospect!'

'For me too!' He eased slightly away from her, fingertips searching out her pulsating core and gently stroking it until she moaned. 'There's no reason why we can't have a rehearsal, though,' he murmured in her ear.

'And then a few charity performances?' she murmured back, mouth lifting in a smile.

'Being such a philanthropic couple,' he added thickly, 'we'll have a nightly performance.'

'No matinees?'

A chuckle escaped him, superseded almost at once by a burgeoning desire that made him thrust into her, awakening her to the glorious peak approaching, the heights of an ecstasy to be reached by love, not merely passion, a love as enduring as Randall's love had always been for her.

'Darling heart!' she cried, sobbing with desire as he exploded within her, and knowing at last that Pearson the Paragon had gone for ever, replaced by the perfect lover, the perfect man, *her* man.

Harlequin Presents

Coming Next Month

1119 COMPARATIVE STRANGERS Sara Craven
Nigel's betrayal had shattered Amanda's dreams of their happy life together.
She doesn't know where to turn until Malory, Nigel's elder brother, takes
charge. He's a virtual stranger to her, yet she finds herself agreeing to
marry him!

1120 LOVE IN A MIST Sandra Field
A disastrous early marriage had brought Sally a small daughter she adored but
left her wary about love and commitment. It was ironic that trying to make a
new start on a holiday on St. Pierre she should meet attractive Luke Sheridan.
He felt exactly the same way she did....

1121 HEART OF THE HAWK Sandra Marton
As a step-aunt with skimpy earnings, Rachel has no legal chance of keeping her
nephew when his wealthy father comes to claim him. She discovers why David
Griffin is called The Hawk—and begins to realize the complications facing her.

1122 TRIAL OF INNOCENCE Anne Mather
Throughout her marriage to Stephen Morley, Robyn kept her guilty secret.
And she has no intention of revealing the truth now—even though Stephen is
dead and his brother, Jared, is asking questions that demand answers!

1123 TOO MUCH TO LOSE Susanne McCarthy
Jessica doesn't deserve her reputation as a scarlet woman, but finds it
impossible to set the record straight. Not that she cares what people think,
especially Sam Ryder. She needs him to save her business—that's the only
reason he's in her life.

1124 TAKE THIS WOMAN Lilian Peake
Kirsten is surprised when she inherits her late employer's country mansion.
She's even more surprised to find herself attracted to his great-nephew, Scott
Baird—especially when Scott wants to ruin all her plans and dreams.

1125 IMPOSSIBLE BARGAIN Patricia Wilson
Money is all that matters to Merissa—for the best of reasons. But Julian
Forrest doesn't know them and promptly jumps to all the wrong conclusions
about her. So why should he want her to pose as his fiancée?

1126 SHADOWS ON BALI Karen van der Zee
Nick Donovan broke Megan's heart two years ago when he plainly rejected her.
Now, meeting again, they're forced to work together on the same project in
Bali. And to Megan's disgust, Nick expects her to behave as if nothing had
happened!

Available in November wherever paperback books are sold, or through
Harlequin Reader Service:

In the U.S.
901 Fuhrmann Blvd.
P.O. Box 1397
Buffalo, N.Y. 14240-1397

In Canada
P.O. Box 603
Fort Erie, Ontario
L2A 5X3

by Leigh Anne Williams

Enter the lives of the Taylor women of Greensdale, Massachusetts, a town where tradition and family mean so much. A story of family, home and love in a New England village.

Don't miss the Taylor House trilogy, starting next month in Harlequin American Romance with #265 *Katherine's Dream*, in October 1988, and followed by #269 *Lydia's Hope* and #273 *Clarissa's Wish* in November and December of 1988.

One house . . . two sisters . . . three generations

TYLRG-1